Fascinated By A Billionaire

A Vampire's Tale

Fatima Munroe

Table of Contents

A Note from Fatima

If you're reading this, I appreciate you for rocking with me. My last book, The Christmas Gift, was my first step out as an independent author, and although the subject matter might not be everyone's cup of tea, I'M proud of it. With this book, I've always been interested in dabbling in urban paranormal, but wasn't sure how I would tell the story. I turned this over and over in my mind for a while before I sat down to write this book. I put it down a few times, picked it up a few times, walked away from it again, came back and finished the story.

There are certain aspects of this book that hit home for me. I think at some point we've all crossed paths with a narcissist, and Charles' character is based on someone who used to be close to me. It took a lot of prayer, tears, and self-validation for me to get past that stage in my life, and this is the last step of my personal healing.

I'd like to thank Vivian Blue, DeeAnn, Kandy Kaine, Hadiya, Thea, Sandra, Kinnie, Loral, Tierra and Unique. A few days before this book released, I had a moment and these beautiful souls reached out to make sure I was ok. I was both humbled and overwhelmed by their love and support and just wanted to shout them all out. I truly appreciate you ladies from the bottom of my heart.

Last but not least, I can't let this book go by without a special shout out to my former publisher. Jah, you've been nothing but amazing for the past four years. I'm grateful to have worked with you and wish you nothing but success as you step into the next phase of your career. Thanks for sharing your knowledge of the industry and advise. You rock!

Subscribe to my mailing list:

http://fatimasbooks.com

Don't forget to leave a review!

Fatima Munroe

Synopsis

Only a vampire can love you forever…

Complacent in her relationships with the opposite sex, Kharynn Lewis spent her days as a flight attendant unknowingly looking for something more. After numerous flings with married men, she longed for the man currently sharing her bed to make good on the promises moaned to her in the heat of passion. Realizing too late she'd never be more than Charles's plaything; she begins to reevaluate her priorities in love and life.

As the head of Bello Enterprises, Vasilios Bello is a charismatic genius who everyone has eyes for, including Cyndi, his personal secretary. Women trip over their feet to be seen on the arm of this corporate shark. Unknown to anyone, including his closest advisor, Vasilios has a deep, dark secret that he's forced to remain vigilant and keep under wraps. Mythical creatures only existed in the fairy tales told to children to keep them afraid at night.

Thrown together while avoiding a potential tragedy, Kharynn can't deny her attraction for the chocolate Olympian who saved her life. In his eyes, Vasilios saw Kharynn as the ultimate temptation: beautiful, voluptuous and inviting. Realizing that their attractions were reciprocated, Kharynn and Vasilios engage in a hypnotic love affair. But once Cyndi and Charles discover their betrayal, will their unpredictable temperaments tear these two lovers apart? He vowed to protect her from harm. She vowed to be his forever. Will their impossible love story be a match made in eternity?

A long time ago…

"Thank you," Vasilios whispered, watching her chest pitch and retreat as she pushed. "I now know you truly love me, this baby has made me the happiest man in all the land."

"I—I AAAHHH!" the blood-curdling scream came from the depths of her soul, running rampant into the sticky Louisiana heat. Underneath the moon's soft and unyielding glow, he could see the sweat drenching her face as she panted, her breath hung thickly in the summer night. A few more pushes and—

"I SEE A HEAD!" the old witch doctor yelled excitedly, perched between the girl's legs patiently watching as her body writhed in pain. "Come on gal! One more push nih!"

"VASILIOS! AAAHHH!" her screeches were closer together now; it was only a matter of time before his first son was born. Created during the still of the fall night, massa's dogs yelped desperately in the distance as they made love nine months ago near the creek and he gave her his seed. She was merely a slave, barely of age, but he had to have her. A timeless beauty such as hers should have a piece of herself forever immortalized to walk with his kind, and once she birthed his son, she would be worthy of—

The crickets chirping loudly outside the one window shack on Old Man Johnson's plantation jerked him out of his thoughts. Surely by now he should be hearing a baby's cry—

"Vasilios, it is God's will," the witch doctor laid a hand gently on his shoulder, nodding her head. Dragging his eyes to the mattress made from straw and old rags, he saw her lifeless body along with that of his only child next to her in peaceful, eternal slumber.

"God's will? GOD'S WILL!" he roared with his head tilted upwards towards the heavens. "WHY DO YOU CONTINUE TO TAUNT ME! Time and time again—"

Almond-shaped eyes briefly flamed a deep crimson red as he morphed from the six-foot four human into his true form. Wrinkles slowly traversed his smooth mocha brown skin; his eyelids drooped further over sunken pupils. Thick eyebrows became caterpillars set midway from his hairline as his nose grew crookedly from its' perch. Opening his mouth to release a long, low hiss, fangs shone in the moonlight as he perched on the makeshift windowsill. Snarling one more time at the stars shimmering brightly as they twinkled far away in the depths of the universe, Vasilios shot the witch doctor an ominous farewell. Limbs stretched to twice the size of his human form, his wingspan touched the tops of the weeping willow trees. With a slight arch of his back, he flew off into the night, never to be seen or heard from again in that lifetime...

Chapter 1

Kharynn

"Good afternoon passengers and welcome to Southwest flight 6213 to New Orleans. Please make sure your seat belts are fastened prior to take off," I recited into the microphone, hearing my voice over the loudspeaker inside the cabin of the Boeing 737. I've been a flight attendant for a few years now, and many a night I'd awakened mumbling these very words in my sleep.

Smiling blankly at the passengers as I continued my spiel, I watched as the other two flight attendants moved up and down the aisle mechanically demonstrating the safety procedures in the event of a water landing. The flight from Raleigh to Atlanta was barely an hour, but as far as I was concerned it may as well have been on the other side of the world. I'd been flying these friendly skies for the past week and a half, and I was ready to go home and put my feet up for the next two days.

Breathing in the stale air from the plane's cabin, pacing back and forth on three or four airplanes a day had a way of taking its toll on a person. Most of my friends saw my life as glamourous mainly because I was getting paid to fly around the world, but I'd happily trade places with them at the drop of a dime. Over the past few months, I began to crave some stability in my life, even if it was just coming home at the end of my day to put my feet up and relax.

"Kharynn, the pilot wants to talk to you," Debra whispered in my ear as I walked past. Smiling curtly at the passengers sitting in first class, I knocked twice and pushed open the door to the cockpit.

"Yes Charles, you wanted to see me?" I spoke as quietly as possible, hoping he didn't hear me. I didn't have the strength to dodge his hands or innuendoes on this flight.

"I uhh…wanted to know why you haven't been returning my calls," he spoke, fiddling with the controls that mapped our flight plan for this trip. "Been trying to spend some time with you for the past three weeks."

But I don't want to spend time with you, I thought, fingering the tiny buttons on my blouse. "I have so many things going on right now that I haven't had a moment to breathe. I'm sorry…"

"No need to apologize, just meet me for drinks at Fogo de Ciao in Buckhead," he continued, unbothered by my hesitation. "That should make up for it."

"Charles, I—,"

"Eight o'clock," he interrupted with his head slightly turned, yet not seeing me roll my peepers at the back of his head. "If I can make time for you, surely you can do the same." Turning back to the view outside the cabin, he unceremoniously dismissed me with a nod of his head.

I took a few moments to collect my thoughts, plastered on my fake smile and stepped back through the door to the main cabin. Knowing there was an airplane full of passengers who depended on me to be pleasant and welcoming as the face of the airline, I continued with my work duties, putting my feelings for what just occurred to the back of my mind. If I wanted to hold on to my sanity, Charles had to go. He was becoming too demanding and I was tired of being one of his many temporary playthings. Even hearing his voice over the loudspeaker announcing that we were approaching Hartsfield-Jackson made me cringe slightly. I couldn't wait until we landed, finally I would be free of him and his overbearing behavior for a little while.

I was partially to blame for his current mood. This was the first time we'd flown together in the past month; when I discovered I was on one of his flights I'd switch and work another schedule. Charles was becoming needy, wanting me to sit with him in the plane's cockpit for most of our trips so he could touch my body without anyone seeing. Which was fine with me, but I could tell the other women on the crew were getting fed up with us playing house when we should have been working. Normally I didn't care what anyone else thought, but with the company rolling out a new 'no-tolerance' policy, I—no we, needed to be more careful of our surroundings.

Charles's voice came across the loudspeaker to announce that we were about to land momentarily. I double checked that our station was clean and neat as Debra walked the aisles one last time for any stray trash or requests from the passengers as we prepared to land. Robotically waving while watching the passengers depart the aircraft, I cringed inwardly when Charles' stray hand conveniently landed on the curve of my backside. I didn't know how I'd gotten to this point in my lifetime, but if I could go back and rewind the past three years for a do-over, I wouldn't be here.

My father left my mother when I was born, and I've always felt as if my mother blamed me for his absence. Sometimes I'd catch her staring at me out of the corner of her eyes with a look of disgust and wondered what I'd done for her to resent me so much. Most of the time my parents didn't know how to talk to each other without yelling and screaming at the top of their lungs, and all my friends were from single parent households. So, when the scholarship letter came the day after prom, it didn't matter to me what it was for; I jumped at the chance to get away from their dysfunctional relationship.

Graduating at the top of my class in high school, I was two and a half years into my residency at Emory when I realized the only reason I was enrolled in the program at all was because I received a full scholarship that I hadn't applied for. My mother was dead set on me being the doctor in the family although I told her I wanted to travel the world for a year before college. I was tired of being told what to do, how to think, and how to live my life. Walking out of Emory in the middle of my clinicals may have been the wrong thing to do, but at the time I could care less. I was doing what I felt was best for me, not what someone else chose for me, and it felt good.

Not having that permanent father figure in my life growing up, I had no idea how relationships worked. In high school, I was the popular girl, and not because of my grades (although I maintained a 4.0 GPA all four years). No, I was the one they whispered about in the girls' locker room; I was the one who allegedly did the band on homecoming weekend. Which I hadn't, but I didn't try to defend myself against the rumors either. So, when I was approached by my college professor during my freshman year asking if I'd like to go out and have a drink, I agreed. One drink turned into one kiss, one kiss turned into one night, and one night turned into a failing grade when I got the abortion behind his back after his wife showed up on campus and made a fool out of both of us.

That incident would've had the average person running to the nearest church to repent, but not me. I dated two more professors and a string of married men after that. I wore the side chick title proudly, because it meant I didn't have to deal with the headache of an actual relationship. Once feelings got involved, I was on to the next one. Charles was a 'happily married' man who had affairs with not just me, but half of the flight attendants based out of Atlanta. But today, for some reason, he was needier than usual; in the past, if I told him no he'd just move on to one of my co-workers. Guess it was my week to be pressed.

I grabbed my luggage from the overhead compartment and dragged my feet as the familiar melody of my suitcase rolled dully along the long halls of Hartsfield-Jackson airport replaying our brief interaction over and over in my head. How was I going to get out of tonight at eight o'clock? Charles had been a pilot with Southwest for at least twenty years, which meant he had the power to get me blackballed on any flight that wasn't his until I met up with him. Although that didn't seem to be his M.O., I'd seen other flight attendants who had been cut down to one day a week for no valid reason although they were considered full time. I could've filed a complaint, but who would take my word over his? I had dug myself into a hole and it was up to me to figure out a way out.

Focusing on the latest web I'd woven with yet another married man, I was deep in thought when I felt eyes staring at my back. Chalking it up to my imagination, I stepped on the train that would take me from the gates to the terminal trying to come up with an excuse that I hadn't used with him yet. Should I say I had to fly home to Dallas to tend to my ailing mother who had been six feet underground for the past year? Or should I fault my non-existent relatives for getting themselves into a mess that I had to drop everything to rush to be by their side?

Tell him you'll be with me, an unknown voice breathed huskily inside my head, interrupting my thoughts. I turned around quickly, ready to snap off on whoever invaded my airspace when I remembered. The person that this voice belonged to would have to be a mind reader, because I hadn't uttered a word aloud. A glance of the crowd proved exactly how tired I was; I was standing in the middle of a train car full of women. Delusions, unfortunately, were an unspoken byproduct of the job; constantly breathing in cabin air for long periods of time on top of a lack of sleep, it was a miracle that we knew our names, much less what time zone we were in at the moment.

"Doors closing." The recorded voice blared over the loudspeaker as the train suddenly leaped forward in a race to the terminal. Absently running my fingers through my hair, I braced myself as the train stopped once we reached the terminal. *I need a nap,* I mumbled softly to myself under my breath, stepping onto the platform heading to the escalator. I'd seen enough airports in the past week to last me for the next couple of months. I'd made up my mind that I'd take these next few days to relax before doing it all over again as if I'd never left.

Vasilios

I had an important meeting and for the first time in years, I was flying commercially since my jet was out of town being serviced. Sitting on the flight from Raleigh to Atlanta wasn't something I was looking forward to, but the brown-complexioned flight attendant made it worthwhile. I didn't want nor need anything from the aircraft staff on such a short flight, but her genuinely pleasant demeanor made the small packet of mixed nuts and bland soda bearable. Her eyes held a mysterious glint that had me mesmerized for the time being; her smile, albeit fake, gave me a strange twinge of joy. I longed to see how her face lit up when she curled her lips upwards on purpose and knew sometime soon my curiosity would be more than just a passing fantasy.

I had a seat in first class and bought the seat next to mine so I didn't have to share an armrest, which meant I had easy access while she tended to my needs. Each time she stood in front of me I was able to drink in her presence for a few seconds longer. Once the plane landed and the other passengers gathered their luggage from the overhead bins, I purposely stood next to her hoping she'd ask if there was anything else I needed, but she smiled and thanked me for flying Southwest before her gaze turned to the person behind me. A man of my stature wasn't accustomed to being blown off, but I maintained my composure for the sake of appearances. I'd been on enough flights in my lifetime to know that I'd see her again soon, so I waited.

It wasn't long before I saw her iridescent mocha skin breeze past my visual for a second time as she walked slowly towards the terminal train on her way out of the airport. Instead of being 'that guy' and following her, I sat back slightly in my seat and watched her walk past me staring straight ahead. Short brown curls bounced slightly atop her head, while her shaved sides were traced into loose pin curls against her ears; her thick, hourglass frame had me temporarily ready to put a ring on it. My nostrils picked up the subtle whiff of her perfume as she strode away, yet at the same time she was so close I could reach out and run my finger across her cheek. Staring at her backside that led down to well-toned legs underneath her skirt, the definition in her calf muscles burned into my memory as she moved away from where I sat admiring her silhouette.

I had to know more about her; what she liked, what she disliked, where she was from…but most importantly why the pilot skimmed the tips of his fingers across the curve in her butt while she waved goodbye to the passengers. Never in all my years had I fallen this hard at first sight…wait…there was one time…but I'd put that memory in a box and tucked back in the far recesses of my mind never to be touched again. There was something almost enigmatic about the flight attendant's aura that I had to know more about, something that drew me to her. Something that made me—

"Oh, excuse me, I am so sorry," I heard only after feeling the cold puddle splash against my chest followed by the strong, putrid smell of American lager. Pushing the thoughts of Kharynn the flight attendant to the side, I focused on the blonde in front of me timidly attempting to wipe the front of my tailored shirt with a napkin from the bar. "My…my hand must've slipped…"

"Don't worry about it," I snatched the napkin from her and proceeded to clean myself up after she dumped a mug of Pilsner on my chest. "Accidents happen."

"I'm…so…sorry…," she grabbed more napkins and began vigorously dabbing the front of my slacks. "Normally I'm not this clumsy."

I realized quickly that her accident was on purpose the more she rubbed her hand across my member, the smile on her face brightening with each stroke. "Thanks, but I'll be fine." I snatched the beer-soaked paper towels from her hands as I stood up. "Try to be more careful next time."

"Oh, so there will be a next time?" her words were full of hope, eyes gleaming with lust as she dragged her hand loosely across her chest.

"Have a good day," I mumbled, gently pushing her away. Heading towards the men's restroom, everything in me wanted to wrap my hand around her neck and squeeze the life out of her for inconveniencing my day, but there were too many witnesses. Normally I resolved my issues with humans deep in the recesses of the night so that no one was around to hear their screams. I derived the ultimate pleasure from their pain, and I knew from the look on the blonde's face that I would have a good night when I showed up at her home unannounced tonight.

Quickly changing my clothes in the bathroom's small stall, I allowed my mind to stay focused on Kharynn, so much so as to embed my intentions into her mind's eye. As an enlightened being who had lived over multiple lifetimes and been exposed to the human mind, there were certain proclivities that I enjoyed that were beyond the average person's understanding. Reading human thoughts and implanting subtle suggestions was more of a hobby of mine back in the 19th century, but I hadn't used that talent since…

Since the day I no longer talk about. The day I don't think about. Since the day I lost…

"DAMN!" I smashed my hand against the mirror, needing to feel the pain to snap me out of my reverie. Pain temporarily distracted me from feeling the human emotions of loss, heartbreak, misery, suffering…pain distracted me from feeling.

From remembering.

From longing.

The night I lost my child was a night that I choose to tuck into the back of my thoughts. I'd been on this earth for almost two hundred years prior to the thought of expanding my bloodline. My father experienced an unfortunate accident that left him on the losing end of a long-fought battle for his own wife's heart from a man on the small island of Lagos, Nigeria before it was considered an island.

After the British invaded our homeland, she was captured and brought to what is now known as the United States as a slave. Once here, my mother ended up becoming a victim of the Salem witch trials in Massachusetts for what her oppressor called witchcraft when she was giving honor to the moon as our ancestors had done for centuries. For that reason, I was in the United States to revenge her death, and after I'd done so, I stayed.

"Bruh, you aight?" a concerned voice came from my right side. "You bleeding."

"Yea, yea I'm good," I collected my thoughts as I turned on the tap on the sink. Blood poured from an open wound in my palm, but the distraction worked. "Just a cut."

"You sho'?"

"Yea, I'm good. Thanks, man." I gave him a brief nod, focusing back on the cut in my hand which was slowly closing on its own.

"Aight," he returned the head nod and disappeared in the world's busiest airport. I briefly flexed my fingers to check for any fragments from the mirror embedded in my skin, satisfied with the knowledge that I was indeed good. Collecting my luggage from the bathroom stall, I headed out and towards the airport exit to climb in my limo with thoughts of Kharynn the flight attendant running indolently through my mind.

Chapter 2

Kharynn

"I don't understand what you want me to do Charles," I sighed frustratedly into the phone's speaker. "My aunt called right after I got off the plane to tell me the family is on their way to Alabama because it's not looking good for my cousin. Am I supposed to tell her no I can't come because Charles and I are meeting for drinks tonight?" I lied angrily. I wasn't in the mood to be bothered tonight. Maybe tomorrow, but not tonight.

"YES! Tell her you got something to do!" he almost bursting my eardrum when he raised his voice at me. "I've already told my wife I'm stuck in California because of the weather so yes! Tonight is my night, dammit!"

I had to mute the phone to stifle a snicker; if he wasn't so serious, he'd be funny. "Charles, I grew up with my cousin Krysse. Our mothers are identical twins; I can't leave my family like that for—"

"I'd do it for you," he pleaded softly in my ear. "Kharynn don't do me like this, I need you tonight. Please."

"Charles—"

"I was gonna wait til later on to tell you this, but," he paused. At that point, I knew I was about to get overdramatic Charles in the next few seconds, "I've decided I'm going to finally do it."

"Do what, Charles?" I stifled a yawn, peeking in my bathroom at the bubble bath patiently awaiting my arrival. Everything in me told me to hang up on this nut and sink into that tub, however, at the moment curiosity was getting the best of me.

"Leaving Eden. I want us to be together, Kharynn. I want us to be a family."

"A family?" *Charles going in for the kill tonight,* I mumbled aloud after muting the phone again so I could get the full yawn out.

"We talked about kids, I don't see any reason why we shouldn't make it official," he continued. "As soon as the divorce is final, we can—"

"Mmm, my aunt is on the other line, I gotta take this," I unmuted the phone so I could get the lie out. He was talking kids, which meant this conversation was over. I don't even like kids. "Can we talk about this when I get back?"

"When is that?" he barked, suddenly agitated.

"I'm not sure yet, lemme see what's going on. I'll call you later, ok?"

"Text me, aight?"

"Ok."

"Don't forget, Kharynn. I wanna know you aight," he pretended like he cared, knowing as soon as I hung up, he'd be calling Debra to see what she was doing tonight. If I cared, I'd pop into Fogo at 8 to see if they were having those 'drinks.' "Text me."

"I will Charles."

"Bye babe."

"Talk to you in a minute," I rushed, hitting end on our call.

I didn't like those lil' pet names that some women needed to validate their relationship with their partner. For what it was worth, Charles and I weren't in a relationship, we had a thing. That thing didn't include good morning texts, 'just because' phone calls, thinking-about-you flowers, trips out of town, date night, or none of those things that couples did. So, when he'd call me those little relationship names like babe, sweetie, love and all that, I ignored it. To this day he hasn't realized his sentiments have yet to be reciprocated. Even during sex, I rarely said anything other than the occasional moan. I had needs and so did he. If we were meeting each other's needs I didn't see the need for us to exchange that cutesy couple banter. *It is what it is.*

After I put my phone on the charger, I headed to the bathroom, stripping out of my clothes as I walked. Stepping unhurriedly down into the garden-sized tub, I smiled slightly because my water was still very warm. Leaning my head back against the tiled wall behind me, I rested my tired orbs and allowed the last week and a half to float out of my thoughts.

Want some company? The voice from earlier on the train mused smoothly through my head, his sweet intonations lodging deep in my psyche. Smooth skin traversed confidently across my shoulder in an unbroken loop; my lips parted blithely with anticipation of his tongue dragging softly across my flesh which never came. Panic seized my movements as my eyes popped open, remembering I was alone in my space. Drunk off of my imagination, common sense kicked me in the gut once I realized I heard a man's voice inside my empty apartment.

"I'm calling the police!" I yelled out to what should have been emptiness, fear lacing my words echoing back to me from the newly interrupted calm. "They come quicker when you down the street from the police station!"

And telling them what? the voice teased. *You hear voices in your head so they should come with guns blazing? Be careful, they might end up taking you for a ride, not me.*

"I must be losing my mind," I spoke aloud, settling back to my comfortable spot in the tub. "Can't be doing ten days straight without a day off no more."

That must be a no then, huh, the deep baritone spoke again. *The things I'd have you screaming just from one touch—*

"Like what?" I decided to indulge my imagination just this once. I had an imaginary friend as a child, maybe he, like me, had grown up.

The voice chuckled smoothly in my mind for a second before it spoke again. *If I was your imaginary friend, we'd already be imaginary married with imaginary kids by now. I'd keep you imaginary pregnant, know that...*

"Tuh," I huffed aloud, wiggling my toes through the thick foamy clouds at my feet. "Imaginary friends don't say stuff like—"

We'll run into each other sooner or later, the voice spoke with that tone that made me want to imaginary stalk him in the daytime with a flashlight. *And I promise your sexy ass won't regret it.*

"We'll see," I smiled to myself at my inner thoughts, wishing by some stroke of luck that he was my reality.

We shall see, the voice spoke for the last time with a cute little man chuckle. I imagined him as a dark hickory colored well-sculpted man with a thick mustache and matching beard. Full lips that spread perfectly across the lower half of his face, his side profile all angles and slopes. Broad chest that sat atop of a pair of rippling abs with a washboard stomach leading down to the V cut of his pelvis. All that and we hadn't even talked about his—

I'm all that plus more, his voice came one last time in my imagination. *Wanna see?*

"Mmhmm…" I heard myself saying as he materialized semi-transparent in my bathroom doorway dressed in a pair of grey sweatpants with no shirt. "Oh my God," softly escaped my lips; my imaginary friend was SEXY!

Come to me, Kharynn, his moans were borderline animalistic as he strode to where I sat nearly submerged in bubbles, water watching his every move.

"Mmhmm."

Now. Right now... he urged in my mind's eye. Leaning in for a second time to whisper in my ear, his transparent lips nibbled against my neck. The touch I craved moments before now meshed against my skin, wrapping my hands around what I hoped was his neck I sensed brute power, unlimited abundance, and eternal success.

"Right now," I wheezed, my mind encompassed nothing more than having this man to myself. There was something about him—something about him was right. Something about him that I craved. Something about him that—

You not ready, Kharynn, he sighed longingly in my ear as I sat moist, ready to consummate our coupling and I didn't even know his name. I'd fallen in love with my imaginary friend who had the body of an Olympian; gave me urges of an ex-lover whose contact I craved— *When you ready, I'll be back.*

"When is that?"

In time. You'll know. Pressing his lips gently against my forehead, my imaginary friend stared deep into my eyes for a few seconds longer, slowly fading from my vision.   "Wait! I know now!" I yelled, my eyes snapping open. My voice echoed back to me as the tepid water and bubbles splashed everywhere. "A dream? He was a damn dream!" I yelled exasperatedly to the shower curtains. Snatching the bar of soap from the soap dish, I lathered my loofah and began to scrub my skin raw, trying desperately to remember his name. "Kharynn, girl you are losing it," I mumbled under my breath before turning on the shower to rinse the soap from my naked skin.

Vasilios

I popped in on Kharynn for a little while before I took advantage of the twilight time to hunt. After the day I had, I needed some entertainment to unwind. I loved Atlanta for that reason and that reason alone: the nightlife. Humans walked the earth inebriated without a care in the world, oblivious to the creatures of the night that preyed on their flesh for nourishment. My first visit, however, was to the blonde from earlier who clumsily dumped a half pitcher of beer on my chest accidentally on purpose for a cheap thrill. Decades had passed since I went out in the world to hunt, but this time it wasn't for sustenance. This time it was personal.

Alighting on the rooftop of the home in Douglasville, I listened to the sounds of her family preparing for their nighttime rest. I wouldn't be here long; my visit was timed for the sole purpose of doing what needed to be done in order to tend to my nightly rounds. The blonde had it coming; maybe her little trick worked on unsuspecting humans in the past, but it wasn't gonna fly with me.

"Goodnight honey," she closed the door to the study, leaving her husband to his own devices as she headed upstairs alone and horny. After she peeked in on her children, I heard her walk the ten steps down the hall to her bedroom and shut the door behind her. Stripping down to her lace bra and panty set that she wore to pique her husband's interest, she climbed tiredly onto the king-sized mattress wistful yet sexually frustrated.

Another night alone, I spoke to her mind as she rubbed her forehead and sighed. *Even your husband doesn't want you.*

"I just need some—wait, who said that?" she bolted upright in her bed, searching her space for the disembodied voice, a body she wouldn't see until it was too late.

You don't remember molesting me earlier at the airport? I materialized semitransparent in the middle of her bedroom, visible just enough for her to recall my face, since it would be the last she'd see. *Told me how clumsy you were while you scrubbed your hand across my—*

"I need to slow down on the wine after dinner," she mused to herself, absently shaking her head.

Oh, I'm very real. I moved methodically towards the blank expression on her face. Vacant blue ocular globes stared fixedly in my direction as my translucent manifestation proceeded deliberately to where she sat in awe. "Still wanna touch me?"

Her slack-jawed expression brought a smile to my face, but I wasn't letting up. Focusing in on her frame, I decided to taunt her amid the torture I knew she was no doubt experiencing from a 'ghost'. As her body quivered helplessly in fear, I could sense the blood that I craved rushing through her veins; her skin flushed with goosebumps. Fear crawled sluggishly across her flesh; her heart thumped violently behind her rib cage. "Who—what are you?"

"I'm your favorite nightmare, Hannah. What I have between my legs is what you wished your husband had," I flirted, dragging my fingertips across her shivering skin. "DO YOU STILL WANT TO TOUCH ME!" I roared harshly in her ear.

"I—I made a bad judgment call," she trembled underneath my touch. "A very bad judgment call that caused you pain—"

"Caused me pain?" I bellowed wildly in her ear. "CAUSED ME PAIN! Do you think that a weak, pathetic, sexually frustrated human such as yourself can cause pain to an immortal being?"

"My husband is coming—" she quivered from my sheer presence; the sweet fragrance of her fear permeated the compacted space between us.

Is he? I whispered in her thoughts. *No one can hear me but you, Hannah.*

"No—" I was thoroughly entertained watching her shake her head vigorously from side to side. "No, he'll be here…I—I hear you loud and clear! Please—RICHARD!"

Touch me. I moved closer still to where she sat on the edge of her bed trying to convince herself I was a figment of her imagination.

"You aren't real—" Hannah slid slowly across the mattress to the middle of the bed.

Touch me, Hannah. I climbed on the bed with her as my face began to transform into my true self.

"N...no," she shivered. Still scooting hurriedly, she quickly landed on her feet on the other side of the bed. I cackled heinously watching her creep timidly towards the bedroom window. "I—I don't want—RICHARD! HELP ME!"

"TOUCH ME HANNAH!" I roared, my intentions vibrating powerfully across the heavens. Lightning flashed throughout the clear indigo sky, the trees bowed slightly from aggressiveness created from my mental utterances, putting the universe on alert. My fangs extended far beyond their usual place behind my lips, glancing at my reflection in her pupils I saw the glow from my own red eyes. Hannah opened her mouth to scream once more, yet the sound of her voice halted forever on her vocal cords. This bitch scared herself to death.

I fell back in the shadows when her husband rushed their bedroom to check on her well-being. He fixated on her frame frozen in fright perched timidly against their bedroom window where she'd decided to jump rather than allow me to torment her for another second. "HANNAH!" he yelped in horror as I licked my chops in the corner, watching him pry her dead fingers from the window's pane. "NO! HANNAH! NOOO!"

Smirking to myself one last time, I filed the sight in front of me into my vast memory bank, alighting on the roof to watch as the police pulled up with sirens blaring. As Hannah's husband tried to explain how he found his healthy wife in their bedroom dead from a heart attack, I looked on with the satisfaction that justice had been served as they slapped handcuffs around his wrists. Had he been doing his husbandly duties, his wife wouldn't have ruined my $650 Hermes button-down shirt, and we wouldn't be at this impasse. He deserved everything he got in my opinion.

One down, two more to go, I mused pensively, extending my wings towards Midtown.

Chapter 3

Kharynn

Damn, I should call him back and tell him it was a false alarm. Despite the lie I told Charles, lying in bed alone was not the move on a Saturday night in Atlanta. Realizing the conversation…dream about a conversation I had with my imaginary friend was the most action I was getting that night was the icing on the cake; I had to be around other people. Even if those other people were drunk.

Debating on whether I should call him or go out alone, I decided on the latter. That way if I wanted to get into something nasty tonight with someone new I could and not feel as if I owed anyone anything. Someone who didn't know me might say something else, but I liked to refer to myself as a free spirit when it came to dating and relationships. I got bored easily, so the thought of being with one person for an extended period scared the hell out of me. It wasn't about the sex, that was what I considered a perk…no it was more about the connection. If I bonded with someone on a higher level than just friendship, I liked having the option to explore and see where that took us.

In the beginning, my attraction to Charles was innocent, yet spawned out of pure curiosity. We didn't initially start as bed buddies; I'd see him in the pilot's lounge between flights and the look on his face told me he needed a friend. We would talk for a while, either in passing or layovers, mainly about his wife and kids, then afterward exchanged contact information. After finding out he was married and considering my track record, I didn't intend on being anything more than a listening ear.

The thing about being in such close quarters for long periods with other people is that it gave us so many opportunities to become something more. Whenever I worked his flights, I made sure he was comfortable, put some eucalyptus oil in the plane's cabin so he didn't have to breathe in stale air...just the little things that I knew he'd been missing at home. At the time he and his wife were on the outs, and she'd tossed out the D word more than once in front of their children. Charles needed some peace, and if he couldn't get it from home, he needed it at work to keep his mind focused with so much responsibility:

"Hey Charles," my heart fluttered seeing his face for the first time in two weeks. "How are you?"

"Hmm?" he turned to stare at me, almost as if he was seeing me for the first time. "Oh, hey Kharynn."

"Awww, what's wrong, friend?" I patted him on the back affectionately, falling in step beside him. That's what friends were for, right?

"Remember when I told you about my wife?" he sighed as we began our journey to the other side of the airport.

"Yeah…" I nodded, eyeing him sideways as we walked side by side through LAX so he would continue his story.

"You ever been tired of a situation, but had no options on how to get out of it?"

"Yes lawd," I chuckled, remembering that pregnancy scare between me and my professor. Thinking back, I might've had that baby had his wife not popped up on campus screaming about how she wasn't divorcing her husband. That incident was the sole reason I didn't want kids. And if I was being honest with myself, I can say I'd fallen in love with her husband; he'd told me on multiple occasions that I could love him so much better than she could. "Don't tell me you're thinking about—"

"I don't know, Kharynn, I don't know," Charles held the door to the lounge open while rubbing the stubble at the base of his hairline. "All I know is that I don't want to be the one to break up our family and have to explain that to my kids. They don't deserve that."

I wished my parents shared his thought process, maybe I wouldn't have found myself in the middle of so many unfortunate predicaments in my lifetime. "No kid deserves that."

"You know sometimes you just need a different perspective on a situation. I think I might take some time to myself to clear my head, you know. No work, no wife, no kids, no decisions to be made, no nagging…just me."

"Sometimes you need that," I agreed. "Couple of days to think."

"So, uhhh…" he paused for a second, then grabbed my wrist, "what you think about going with me?"

"Going with you?" I tried to remove myself as he applied a little pressure, "Going with you where?"

"Cali…Costa Rica…Puerto Vallarta…where you wanna go, love?" he smirked boyishly.

"I—I don't know, Charles," I scrutinized the room moving my head side to side to see who might be listening in on our conversation. "People talk."

"We ain't gotta fly Southwest," he whispered. "We work for an airline, I'll jump seat a few tickets on Delta so we can go," his fingers ran carelessly up and down my arm as he spoke. Something in his voice was tempting, he had my curiosity piqued…a few tickets to where?

Staring at a married man who I realized was making me an indecent proposal and I was stuck. This happened to other people, not me. Who wouldn't jump at the chance to travel the world? The potential to be spread-eagled on a white sandy beach with the sun beating down on my carob skin was the opportunity I dreamed of since I was old enough to dream. But this…this with Charles of all people…we worked together…he was the captain of the plane. He made sure we were safe, transported strangers from one place to *another on a strict schedule. And now that same man wanted to stop the world so we could get off and get lost somewhere in the ether…*

"What time do we leave?" I smiled brightly, looking forward to our trip.

My fingertips slid gently against my lips during my trip down memory lane, Charles was such a hopeless romantic in the beginning. Our five-day mini-vacation to Santorini, Greece was the first of many; my passport was full of stamps from around the world thanks to him.

But the more time I spent with him, the worse I felt for his wife. In these types of situations, I was the one who moved in the shadows, regulated to a luxury hotel room with a standing reservation for a weekend day. I was the one whose phone number remained cloaked under a pseudonym, the one who 'he' came to see when he suddenly received an urgent phone call that he had to take care of immediately. I was the one who turned her head to the side when 'he' was spotted by mutual friends, the one who pretended that I didn't know THIS man whose name I'd screamed to the rooftops as I spelled mine across his naked pelvis.

I met Charles's wife and kids during a Christmas party, and they were adorable. His wife Eden was a beautiful woman, and their two girls were the cutest little princesses. For him to risk that…for him to throw that away for someone who didn't even want kids…I couldn't. I couldn't allow him to do that.

Over the past few months, Charles hadn't noticed that I was now busy on those hotel nights. It was easy; I picked up a few extra shifts under the guise of needing to pay down my student loan debt to buy a house. As much as he insisted he could help out, I refused. Now knowing all those trips we took somehow took away from him providing support for his family made me nauseous. I wondered what kind of Christmas those brown-eyed beauties had while their father was showering me with money, purses, and diamonds that I refused to take.

Now with the holiday season slowing down, I was struggling to pick up any shifts. Only after talking to another flight attendant who'd been out for a while dealing with a family issue did I come up with using that same idea with him. It worked the first few times, but now…we'd talked too much about ourselves for me to give such a flimsy excuse.

Maybe I won't call him. Maybe we don't have anything to discuss. Maybe I was being hopeful, grasping at straws…hoping he'd get fed up with my excuses. Hoping he'd realize that us having a kid wouldn't keep me in his life. Hoping he'd—

KNOCK, KNOCK, KNOCK…What the…

"Kharynn, open this door! I already saw your car outside!" Charles's voice barked from the other side of the oak door.

Even after my little reminisce party, I had to remain firm; he and I wouldn't be spending THIS night together or otherwise.

Ignoring his urgent knock, I sat on my bed and scrolled through Facebook for a while to see what my friends were doing as his fist continued to connect with the dense wood. *Oh, they went to the New Edition concert, huh. I ain't get an invite,* my face scrunched up while opening the pics and videos my friends posted online.

"Oh, I must be interrupting, huh," he chuckled snidely from the hallway outside my door. "Hmph. I understand. Yeah, I understand completely. Too good to climb out of, ain't it bruh. Next time just let me know, maybe we could've had a little party or something. Aye, I ain't mad at all," he called out childishly. *Aww. His little pride bruised. That's cute,* I smirked to myself. Where was my imaginary friend so we could laugh at this clown?

Vasilios

They were drunk, the group of women teetering down Peachtree were all barely dressed and had no idea where they parked their car. So free…without a care in the world…I loved how alcohol lowered these humans' inhibitions and made them feel invincible. *Nothing bad happens to you when you're drunk*, I overheard one of them cackle as a second threw up on the sidewalk.

I fell in step behind the young women who couldn't be older than 32, stifling a chuckle as the tall one tripped over her own feet. She just missed face planting herself into the concrete in front of her. Another of her friends started crying helplessly at the near-miss, and they all crowded around her, even the clumsy one. *This was too easy*, I smirked seeing them all crouched on the ground in the opaque parking lot with no one around. Rounding the corner, I raised a hand with claws extended when I heard it.

HER.

Kharynn needed me. She didn't know that in that accidental meeting on the plane and subsequent home encounter, we were now soul mates. I knew it; she'd stirred feelings in me that I'd allowed to remain dormant for centuries. Those feelings of want, need…longing for her touch. Strands of her perfumed hair gently pressed against my chest as she slept after a night of passionate intimacy; her smooth hickory-colored skin the opposite of my tawny hue. But…she didn't even know my name.

It was time to change that.

*

The temperature in the city was warm, considering it was the end of February. Atlanta weather was funny like that; it could snow a half-inch one day and the next it would be 75 degrees and sunny. Instead of grabbing an unsuspecting victim from the club, I decided to get closer to her. Knowing my impatient nature, I didn't want to wait until I ran into her for a second time.

I was sitting at a table in the corner at the Waffle House down the street from her apartment watching her shape walk through those glass doors. In her uniform she was sexy, but here...like this...damn. Kharynn wore a white t-shirt with form-fitting navy blue jogging pants, and a pair of grey, white and canary yellow Air Max adorning her petite feet. The curls were combed out of her pixie cut with all of her hair pulled loosely to the back of her head. "Maxine, I need an All-Star like ASAP," she ordered, flopping down at the counter.

"Another one of those weeks, huh Kharynn," the lady behind the counter, who I assumed was this Maxine person, sprang into action on the grill. "What happened this time?"

"You'd think the fact that we have a union would guarantee me forty hours as a full-time employee, right," Kharynn grumbled, fiddling with the menus shoved down inside the napkin holder. "Girl, they only scheduled me for three DAYS. Then when I go to my union rep and let him know, he gave me that line about cutbacks and everybody going through something, not just me. Yet and still, HIS schedule looks just fine." She flung the menu across the almost empty restaurant.

"Yea, I hate it when the manager make it seem like everybody in the whole company struggling, knowing it's just the little people," Maxine agreed, pouring her a cup of coffee. "They don't care about whether or not you making rent or if the lights cut off, all they care about is money. Miss a shift because you got business to take care of and see how fast they let you go though!"

"I'm 'bout to go look for another job because this ain't it," Kharynn mumbled as she dumped white granulated crystals of sugar spoon by spoon into the steaming hot cup of caffeine. "I give that job so much of my time and for what? Free flights? Hell, I can barely use them; when I got the money I'm scheduled to work and when I'm broke, I can't go nowhere!"

"Ain't that the truth!" Maxine continued to flip the waffle iron with one hand while the other filled a small saucer with pats of butter. Piling piping hot food onto a porcelain dish, she slid the plate across the counter, which slowed to a stop in front of my future wife.

"You know what we need, girl?" Kharynn promptly snapped up a piece of bacon from her plate, using the crispy meat to emphasize her point. "Somebody that's gonna take care of us so we don't have to be bothered with this nonsense from these jobs."

"Mhmm, a rich man," Maxine agreed. "But he can't be ugly, and he gotta know how to keep his hands to himself. You know when a lot of these men get money they start beating on these women, then try and make them sign a non-disclosure agreement so people don't know what a world-class asshole they are."

"I know that's right!" Kharynn poured syrup on her waffles, dissecting each one into neat little triangles. "Whatever happened to that 'happily ever after' love that Snow White and Cinderella had? I mean, it had to have existed somewhere, right? You can't write about something that you've never been through unless you've been through it, right?"

Maxine wiped her hands on her apron as she faced Kharynn, staring at her just as crazily as I was from my spot in the corner. "Girl, what?"

"Nothing. You know I start hallucinating after midnight," she cackled, turning back to her food.

Both women laughed before Maxine remembered I was there. "But you know who…" she dropped her voice to whisper, not knowing I was still able to hear her words, "…is sexy as hell? That man back there in the corner. Yea, he came in here right when you did, ordered a coffee and been sitting there ever since. Why don't you go introduce yourself to him?"

"You just gonna pawn me off to a total stranger, huh. I thought you was my girl," Kharynn darted her smoky orbs back and forth between me and Maxine.

"I am. And as your girl, it's my job to make sure you good," she reasoned. "Plus, I'm not his type, you are."

"How you know?"

"He ain't looked at me twice since he been here, but he been watching you since you stepped out your car. Gon' head see what he say, if I'm wrong then it's no love lost. But if I'm right, name your first daughter Maxine," she giggled, nudging her friend.

"Wait, I'm supposed to go say something to him? Girl, naw," Kharynn waved her off with another piece of bacon. "If he been eyeballing me, then he gotta make the move. I'm a lady first."

I took her cue; first dusting the imaginary crumbs from my tailored slacks. Dabbing any moistness from the corners of my lips with a napkin, I grabbed my keys from their spot next to the saucer near my cup and headed towards both women. Allowing my gaze to rest a little longer on Kharynn's features, I gave both women a welcoming smile. "Uhmm, excuse me miss."

Maxine nudged Kharynn, who sat up a little straighter on the stool as they both waited expectantly for my next words. "Yes?"

"I'm not sure how these things go, seeing as how I'm new here…"

"Just say what you mean." Maxine and Kharynn exchanged knowing glances between smirks.

"I need to get going, and since you didn't come to my table with the check…" I purposely fidgeted with my keys, amused at the matching embarrassed frown on both of their faces.

"Oh, uhhh…" Maxine rushed the cash register while Kharynn took a long sip from her coffee mug. "Right here."

I dug in my pocket for my wallet; fishing around for my credit card while Kharynn's eyes pierced through my soul. "Excuse me, sir. I don't mean to be rude, but you look so familiar to me. Do I know you?"

"Depends." I passed my card to Maxine and waited for the approval for my drink. "Have you been to Mercedes-Benz stadium lately?"

"No…wait…"

"My team of architects designed the structure, and the construction side of my company was responsible for the framework," I spoke, signing the credit card slip. "Maybe you've heard of Bello Enterprises? Parent company of the hottest urban network since the old BET?"

"Uhmm…no."

"In that case…" I dropped a fifty-dollar bill on the counter for Maxine's tip, "maybe I just have one of those familiar faces.

Enjoy your evening ladies." Nodding in their direction, I smiled once more at Kharynn's flustered expression.

I blinked the car's lights from my key fob, briefly illuminating the plate glass window of the restaurant. The quick blare of the horn broke the 2 a.m. silence echoing throughout the surrounding neighborhood while I lowered myself into the vehicle's muted interior. With the tint on my windows a shade darker than legal, I smirked watching Kharynn and Maxine as they gossiped about me to each other. *Damn, she was even sexier when she was mad!*

I hit the push-button start and was about to pull out of my parking spot when another car skidded into the spot next to mine. The driver hopped out and made a beeline for the front door, hastily shoving his hands in his pockets. Bulldozing his way inside, he removed his hands from his pockets, producing something black in the process. I could hear both women screaming, Kharynn's panicked yelps shot right through me, her fear of the situation gave me even more motivation.

"Please don't shoot, I'll give you the money," Maxine fumbled over the register's buttons, trying to pop it open. I shoved the door out of my way and knocked the slim man to his knees with a loud thud. Kharynn was completely unaware of the gun as it slid across the floor and stopped right at her feet.

"The hell wrong with you, man?" I roared, kicking the aspiring felon in his ribs. "You come in here to rob two women? TWO WOMEN?"

"You think I care about two lonely bitches?" he screamed, squirming under my foot. "Aye, empty the damn register!"

"Kharynn, Maxine, go stand in that corner while I handle this little situation, ok?" I instructed, making sure they were both out of harm's way in case he had another weapon. Once they complied, I leaned down to whisper in his ear so the women didn't hear the few words he wouldn't forget anytime soon. "If this was another time, maybe another place, I'd rip your head off your shoulders and feed your worthless remains to the dogs," I spat in his ear. "But since there are witnesses, I'll let you off with a warning: stay out of dark alleys at night." I picked him up by his neck and tossed him haphazardly into the door. "My bad bruh, lemme get that for you."

"AAAHHH!" he yelped once his body met the concrete sidewalk from being out. I walked back inside to wash my hands first, then went back to the counter to check on the women.

"Thank you so much!" Maxine and Kharynn rushed to where I was perched on the stool. "He's been in here so much my boss threatened to fire me if I got robbed again!"

"Shouldn't a man be working here with you? You ain't got no business in here alone at night," I scolded, texting my contact at the police station while Kharynn patted my shoulder. "And what about you? Shouldn't you be at home?"

"Yea, but—wait a minute," she paused for a second. "How do you know our names?"

"Excuse me?" I'd just saved them both from being robbed and she was worried about how I knew who she was?

"I said how do you know our names?" she tried to stare through me, waiting for my response.

"You yelled her name when you walked in and she replied with yours. Your voice reminded me of someone I used to know, naturally I'd look up to see if you were she." I replied cooly without hesitation. "Not to mention there's something about you that intrigued me, I gotta admit I was a little curious."

"About me?" she blushed.

"Yes, about you." I tucked two fingers underneath her chin to lift her head so I could look into those haunting brown orbs. I tilted her head slightly; the soapy scent of her clean skin triggered the memory of her naked body amidst the frothy bubbles in her bathroom. "You not ready for me yet, Kharynn."

"I—I'm sorry, I have a boyfriend …"

"Boyfriend, huh." I chuckled to myself. "Woman like you need a husband if you ask me," I murmured playfully near her earlobe.

Meet me at your place, I spoke telepathically in her head while my lips said, "I'll make a call to a friend of mine on the force and have them circle the neighborhood. You really shouldn't be here alone Maxine. Nice to meet you, ladies."

"Thanks again—I'm sorry, I didn't catch your name," Maxine called out behind me.

"Vasilios. Vasilios Bello." I formally introduced myself to both women. "By the way, if your employer decides to release you for this or any other incident in the future, give me a call." I pressed two of my cards into her outstretched hand.

Vasilios Bello, Kharynn thought, silently leering in my direction. My keen senses picked up on her lecherous thoughts coupled with the subtle sweet scent emanating from between her thighs. "So, are you from here Mr. Bello?" her mind struggled to form those words alone. I knew what she REALLY wanted to ask, but I held my tongue.

"My family is from Nigeria, but my company is headquartered in Midtown near 13th and Peachtree." I answered as humble as I could, considering. I never wanted to be that rich guy that everyone bowed at his feet I was just as comfortable at Waffle House as I was at Ruth's Chris.

"Peachtree Street?" Maxine spoke up, oblivious to the sexual tension between me and her customer/friend. "Been trying to get a job down there for years!"

"Give my assistant a call, I'm sure we can find a spot for you," I spoke, peering outside. "There's the first car. You should see someone from patrol circling this block every fifteen minutes. Don't forget that call to my office tomorrow, ok?"

"I will, Mr. Bello. Thank you again!"

I glanced over at Kharynn to see where her head was, picking up on latent thoughts of her and the pilot from the flight earlier. As I watched, a chill shivered through her body, rattling her out of her thoughts. *Go home,* I urged mentally.

"Maxine I'm 'bout to head out." She stared at me a little longer, tossing a few bills on the counter. "That's enough action for me tonight."

"Let me make sure you make it to your car," I volunteered. "Just in case that guy is circling the block, I need to make sure you're safe."

"Are you always a gentleman?" Her hips swayed side to side hypnotically as she sashayed through the restaurant's threshold.

"Is there any other way to be?" I ushered her to her car, patiently watching her unlock the door to lower herself in. "Not all men are savages, it's still a few of us in the world."

"Us?"

Vampires. "Gentlemen." I smiled respectfully. "Do you need an escort home this evening?"

"Uhmm, no thank you, I think I'll be ok," she blushed a second time. "Thanks, Mr. Bello."

"Not a problem, Kharynn. Take care." Tapping the roof of her car twice, I watched her back cautiously out of the small parking lot and pull into the street. I waited until her taillights disappeared down the street, then got in my vehicle and headed in the opposite direction to park my car in the building's garage. It wouldn't take long for me to make it to her place.

Chapter 4

Kharynn

"Vasilios Bello," I repeated his name over and over on the drive to my apartment. His name…the mere syllables felt smooth against my tongue and rolled off my lips with ease. I only lived a few blocks from the Waffle House, so it didn't take long for me to make it home. Parking in my designated spot, I rushed upstairs and into my apartment, still a little scared but giddy with excitement thinking about the stranger who turned into my hero in a matter of moments.

When the robber initially burst into the diner with that gun in hand, for a split second I thought Charles had followed me. Staring in those vacant eyes, hearing his voice echo through my ears as he demanded Maxine open the register, I sat helpless, secretly hoping Vasilios would come back to save me. Lo and behold, my wish came true in a matter of moments; my savior burst through those doors like a mocha Superman to save my day, my week, my month, my entire life! I didn't know how to thank him, but certain parts of my body had a few ideas of her own.

I knew I was tired; as we thanked him for his chivalrous actions, I could've sworn I heard his voice in my head urging me to go home. After kissing Maxine on the cheek with a promise to call, I did as I was told. Arriving at the place I'd called home for the past four years, my keys landed atop the table next to the front door. I kicked my shoes onto the welcome mat as I floated around my apartment in a daze. I recognized my imaginary friend in the flesh when I shifted my gaze to the booth on my right side at the restaurant. The whole situation was baffling; one minute I was in bed daydreaming about the dream I had in the tub, then the next I was throwing on something quick to get something to eat. It was almost…fate.

I shot Maxine a quick text to let her know I made it home. Stripping out of my shirt and pants, I buried my head underneath the down comforter until sleep wrapped me up in her gentle arms. Praying that Vasilios visited me in my…

Kharynn, his voice inside my private thoughts breathed life into my lethargic soul. *Thinking about me again I see.*

"I'm—I'm not…" The temperature in my bedroom shot up at least ten degrees, sweat beaded against my lip as my chest pitched and fell. "How did you get in my apartment?"

I'm here, he whispered as a cool breeze roamed across my chest. *Let me whisper my intentions into your erotic, I want you to feel needed, let me make you feel secure here…with me.*

"Vasilios…"

I want you Kharynn. I. WANT. YOU…

His words came right on time; but too late. I had a type: married, engaged or otherwise involved. From what I could tell,

Vasilios was neither. However, there was a familiarity about him that my soul craved, that I longed to be near and entangled between. From our brief meeting, I knew I wanted to be wrapped up in Vasilios for the rest of our days, whether it was in love, marriage, or if we were just shacking up. Before I went into a new situation, I had to get out of an old situation. A situation with a married man that I had no business sneaking off with, no business doing anything other than the basic hello, goodbye and occasional small chat.

Charles' marriage didn't have a chance because of me. I take that back because cheating is a conscious choice made by a person otherwise in a committed relationship who chooses to go outside of that relationship for…for what? According to Charles, it was because his feelings changed, he wasn't happy. And since his feelings changed, he wasn't sure if he should be involved in a relationship that was built on an unstable foundation. None of which had to do with me.

I had to do this. For myself, for my sanity, for ME. Most importantly…for Vasilios.

*

"Mmm…" I sighed, searching through the covers for my ringing phone as the sun's rays peeked through the blinds. "Hello?"

"Oh, so he finally let you answer the phone, huh," Charles hissed in my ear.

I took a deep breath in and exhaled, ready for this conversation to happen. Knowing this man was about to scrape across my last nerve first thing in the morning, I massaged my temple with one hand, propping the phone between my shoulder and my ear. "Who is 'he', Charles."

"You know who he is," Charles huffed bitterly. "The brotha who made you lie to me so you could sneak him in this house."

"Sneak? You don't pay any bills here! Who I bring to MY house is MY business!" I yelled angrily, fully awake.

"If that's the case, why you lie?" he challenged. "I know you were here last night, I heard you moaning his name when I came by! 'Oh…Steve…Steve,'" he whined stupidly in my ear in a lame attempt at mocking me. "I heard you tell him to be quiet when I knocked! You didn't think I listened at your door?"

"Steve? Who the hell is Steve, Charles?" I taunted because he was being childish, yet again. And to think Southwest trusted this eight-year-old trapped in a grown man's body with an aircraft full of people.

"Kharynn you KNOW who Steve…why are you doing this to me? Huh? Why do you do these things to me knowing how I feel about you?" he whined.

"What am I doing to you?" Now I was confused.

"You always do this! You do all these things to get my attention, then once you get it and I give you what you wanted, you start acting like you wanna be in a relationship! You know my situation…"

"Your situation?" I was beginning to feel the heat rise in my chest. "Charles, you're married. That's a little more than a situation."

"…and then when I tell you I choose you over her, now you want somebody else? Why lead me on, Kharynn? Just call this what it is…"

"You CHOOSE me? You know what, you're right. Let's call this what it is! I want sex! You were offering, so I took it! Don't blame me because you don't know the difference! And then you got a whole wife and kids…did you not notice how I been trying to pull away from you for the past four months? Of course, you didn't! You're way too selfish to have noticed! And now you choose me? Tuh! You and Eden need a marriage counselor, a pastor, and Jesus, honey I'm not trying to be a part of that! Then you got the nerve to say you want a kid by me? Did you forget that you have two already? Gave me what I wanted? DON'T FLATTER YOURSELF! I got vibrators that make me scream louder than you! I just like skin on skin sometimes, but please! Don't do me no favors!"

"You know what. I'm not doing this with you. I got enough on my plate with a wife who doesn't want me to touch her, kids who barely know who I am…I ain't got time to coddle yo' ass too! IT'S

OVER!" he roared. The phone slammed against something hard and our call disconnected. Once again, Charles was pissed at his overactive imagination and I was the one paying for it. The good news was we were done.

"It's over." I breathed a sigh of relief for my freedom. Relief washed over me like cleansing summer rain; no longer would I be subjected to the sideways glances from my co-workers, no longer would I have to put up with the condescending smiles followed by acrid whispers once I left the room. No longer was I tethered to the whims of a pompous, arrogant, egotistical, narcissistic adulterer who felt I had to check in with him every hour of my life because we were in a situationship.

I blinked my surroundings clear, rubbed my eyes and rolled out of bed. Heading to the bathroom, I relieved myself, washed my hands and brushed my teeth. Once finished, I hopped in the shower to freshen up before I started my day. There was a thing going on at Piedmont Park that I'd thought about going to, but the thought that Charles' wife might be there with the kids…maybe not. However, he was allegedly in California stuck in 'bad weather'.

Why was I so enamored by him? Was it his looks? Did I have a thing for men with power? Or was it the fact that he flew an aircraft with ease, that power…

Power. Just like that, Vasilios's voice eased into my thoughts comforting my nerves, subsequently calming my senses. *I want to taste your lips, Kharynn.*

His voice always came through at the perfect times: right before bed, right after I dealt with Charles and his foolishness, during my quiet and alone times. Somewhere deep in my psyche, I wanted him here with me, sharing his airspace. *Which ones?* I chided playfully to the voice in my head.

With the right person, there is no such thing as a right or wrong pair of lips, I imagined his lustful response. *Let me slurp that girl for you...French kiss you between your thighs...graze my teeth gently across your lower lips then slide my tongue inside, slurping on the juices of your emotions...Kharynn I need you...*

"Vasilios..." I slid down the door to my bedroom in slow motion, the words I wanted to hear formed in his throat and watch leave his lips...HIS words formed in my mental made my knees weak.

Do you feel my hand on your neck, Kharynn? That gentle squeeze is me applying pressure...I can feel the moan stuck in your larynx...that shiver coming from your left thigh...your heart beats five beats faster because you're thinking of me, knowing how only I can give you the things that you've spent years chasing...

"What's that, love?" Mentally I was consumed by my pool of wanton desire for a man who I'd just met a few hours ago.

Love... I felt the cool breeze against my neck, symbolizing his lips against my flesh, *loyalty*... the breeze whispered ever so softly as it traveled slowly across my neck, *and orgasms,* the breeze settled in the crevice between my ample breasts.

"Love, humpf," I snorted. "What's that?"

Love is giving someone the power to destroy you, but trusting that they won't, the whisper echoed through my brain. *Not just good sex.*

Damn, I never thought of love like that. "You know what they say about good sex: it's pointless if you can't have meaningful conversation naked and eating a bag of chocolate-covered pretzels, babe."

And food. I gotta feed my baby, he chuckled, inciting vivid thoughts of lovemaking through my body.

Charles promised me all those same things, so I was hesitant—

I'm not Charles, Vasilios's acrid tone interrupted my brief dwell on the past. *Real men are honest, real men live in their truth no matter how much that truth hurts. Don't compare me to that asshole.*

My eyes popped open again like they always did when he inundated my thoughts. "I must've been asleep." Right?

If that's what you tell yourself, Kharynn. Like I said before, you not ready for me, Vasilios's voice echoed as my phone rang. "Hello?"

"Hey, Kharynn Lewis?"

"Speaking, who's calling?"

"Yes, Ms. Lewis this is John Farr, your union rep. I was giving you a call to inform you that we're doing some cutbacks and the company has decided to do some layoffs. As your flight crew has more seniority, we have decided to place you on furlough for the next six weeks. Your working hours for the month have been reassigned, however, you are on standby in the event that one of your peers in unable to report for duty."

"For the next six weeks?" I gripped the phone confused. Never, in the four years that I worked for Southwest; had I been furloughed. Business was booming, Southwest stock was through the roof, literally. "Is this a paid leave?"

"Well if it was paid, we wouldn't need to furlough the staff," Mr. Farr sneered crudely.

"What am I supposed to do for rent? How am I supposed to live?" I demanded to know, refusing to allow the tears pooled in the crevice of my orbs to fall. How convenient that once Charles decided we were done, now suddenly I was being furloughed?

"I'm not sure Ms. Lewis, but the decision has been made. Do you know anyone with children? Maybe you can babysit or do some odd jobs for money. Call a friend and get a loan."

If that ain't the dumbest— "Thank you for the call, Mr. Farr. Enjoy the rest of your day." I hung up so I didn't hear his reply. Babysit? Odd jobs? I was surprised he didn't suggest I get a paper route. Babysitting and odd jobs would barely cover my light bill, much less my rent.

I dropped my head in my hands and allowed the tears seeping from my pupils the release they deserved. I knew what I was getting myself into by falling for a married man, but I never thought he would take his little retaliation game this far. Getting me laid off my job? We went from him licking my vagina in the cockpit to practically fired in a matter of twenty-four hours.

Bello Enterprises was beginning to sound like the odd job that I needed to stay afloat for the next six weeks. Vasilios gave both of us his card last night, and I was sure I dropped it somewhere in my bag. Dumping everything in the middle of my king-sized bed, I fished out his information and gave him a call.

Vasilios

"So, as you can see from the figures, last year the company posted profits in all areas with the exception of…" I half-listened to the accounting department's presentation. My main reason for coming to Atlanta in the middle of the week was because the board decided at the last minute to have the annual disclosure meeting before providing the information to the public. I already had the reports at my fingertips and reviewed them daily; my being at the physical meetings was a formality.

My secretary peeked her head in and interrupted our meeting, winking in my direction. "Excuse me gentlemen, but Mr. Bello has a call on line 562 and the caller says it's important. Do you want me to take a message?"

"No, I'll take it in my office," I stood up and buttoned my suit coat, giving everyone at the table a polite nod. "Gimme a few minutes and transfer the call, Cyndi."

"Yes sir, Mr. Bello."

I strode to my office with a slight smirk on my face, listening to Kharynn's moans while I entertained myself to break up the monotony of the day had me feeling nostalgic. A man of my stature who lived over many lifetimes, my experiences with the female form was both vast and lascivious. It would be easy for me to take her, convince her that her submitting to my whims was of her own volition as I had done so many times in the past. That's not what I wanted with her, not who I wanted to be for her. I didn't just want her, I needed her. I wanted to kiss her voluptuous lips over and over every day, I wanted to laugh with her, nourish her. Ever since yesterday on the plane, I realized something I couldn't quite put my finger on when it came to Kharynn: I missed her.

"Bello." I smoothed my tie down as I sat on the corner of my desk. My corner office that overlooked the city of Atlanta from the 45th floor resonated with my true self, and I enjoyed the feeling of asserting my authority over the city's unsuspecting residents.

"Hi…uhmm Vasilios?"

Every fiber of my being tingled hearing her voice on the other end. In the brief time I'd known her, I felt like I knew everything about her, including the pitch in her voice when she was nervous. "Yes, Vasilios speaking."

"Hi…uhmm yes…I'm not sure if you remember me from last night, but…"

"Kharynn. Yes, I remember you. How can I help you?"

"Oh wow," she giggled nervously. "I didn't think you'd know who I was. But yea…you said if I needed a job to give you a call…"

"Of course."

"Uhmm…do you…do you have anything part-time maybe? I just need something temporary."

"We don't have anything temporary. I prefer my staff to be well versed in all areas of the company; a temp wouldn't know anything about quarterly earnings or press releases." I automatically switched into business mode. "What happened to the airlines?"

"How did you know…"

"After we parted ways, I remembered you were the flight attendant on my trip yesterday," I smiled, ready with a reply. "Raleigh to Atlanta? I was the guy sitting by myself in the first row on an overbooked flight."

"That's right, you were! I knew you looked familiar last night!" she chuckled heartily. "You know I almost got wrote up because of your empty seat?"

"Well, I did buy both tickets, so it wasn't exactly your fault," I pulled the chair out from my desk and sat down. "Called my buddy over at Southwest and told them to give you a raise because of your impeccable service, did they call you?"

"Yea, they called me all right," her voice dropped into her chest, I could almost see her facial expression change. "Told me I was being furloughed for six weeks, that's why I'm calling you now."

"What? Says who?"

"My union rep called me a few minutes ago. Said I should find an 'odd job' when I asked how I was supposed to live," she sighed. "I'm sorry to be telling you my problems, none of this has anything to do with you and I don't want to be the charity hire."

"So, after all that, you still want to stay there?" I rubbed my chin, lost in thought. I could move Cyndi down the hall to work with one of the VP's and have Kharynn come work with me for the time being. It would be a win/win for me, I'd work in close proximity of that body every day. Staying Atlanta for a while was beginning to sound more and more appealing.

"I mean, I'm not exactly looking to leave Southwest permanently, I just need something for right now. They have great benefits, not to mention free flights," she giggled.

"Well, that's understandable. Stop by the office and we'll go through the particulars. When do you want to start?"

"Huh? Wait, you have something for me?"

"Of course. Someone with your people skills would be an asset to any company. We'll find a spot for you." I shuffled a few folders on my desk, my eyes landing on the one with a stack of pamphlets inside. "I'll be here until around 4, so if you can come in between now and 3, that'll be ideal."

"Thank you so much Vasilios," she gushed happily. "You won't be disappointed!"

I'm sure I won't. "Not a problem, Kharynn. See you soon." I waited until she hung up then turned my attention to the folder full of literature from apartment complexes in Midtown. "Cyndi, can you come in here a second?"

"Hey Vasilios," she walked in my office with an award-winning smile. "I see you got my little package."

"What's this?"

"Last time we were together you said you wished we were in the same city together so we could spend more time getting to know each other," she cooed seductively. "I got those so we can go look at some places."

"What?"

"I—isn't that what you wanted?" she seemed genuinely confused.

"Cyndi, get me a listing of everyone who works in this building along with their job titles and rate of pay. And take this with you." I shoved the booklets in her direction, dismissing her.

"Vasilios—"

"You know, I'm racking my mind trying to remember when I told you it was ok for you to refer to me as anything other than Mr. Bello," I swiveled slowly in my leather seat to look out at the traffic beginning to subside on the southbound lanes of I-85. For me to have had less than a few hours of sleep, I was feeling refreshed and revived, and I knew it was because of Kharynn. "Are you still in my office?"

"No need to be so harsh, Vasilios," Cyndi huffed, her footfalls moving away from my desk. "I've always—"

"Hated your job and looked forward to being terminated? No sense in prolonging the inevitable," I interrupted.

"My apologies, Mr. Bello," she cleared her throat as the door opened. "I'll get you those files right now." She seemed reserved for a change, a far cry from her assertive tone a few seconds ago.

I felt around my desk until my hand landed on the case that held the titanium stress balls that I used for when I felt a little tension in my shoulders. Removing the trinkets from their case, I held both in the palm of my hand, rotating the reflective orbs counterclockwise to help me think. I closed my eyes and allowed my mind to wander back to the night I blurred the line between employer and employee with my secretary:

One weekend after third-quarter earnings posted to my accounts, I decided to go out to celebrate. Not wanting to be surrounded by a bunch of out of towners, I went to a place in the suburbs that I'd heard about from one of my colleagues. Stepping inside the dimly lit space, I saw champagne and other alcoholic beverages flowing freely at the bar. Strangers bounced and shook their inhibitions away to the pounding bass coming from the DJ booth on a hot Atlanta evening. Finding myself a seat at the bar, I was positive I wouldn't be recognized by anyone; my goal was to blend into the sea of nameless strangers while I did some people watching.

After a couple of shots of bourbon, I had a vibe going, so imagine my surprise when I saw my secretary Cyndi step inside the club. With her bone straight hair fanned across her bare shoulders, she wore a sheer halter top that looked good painted on her thick frame. When we finally locked eyes, I knew for a fact I was gonna take advantage of the situation.

"Mr. Bello," she purred, stroking her fingertips across the bulging veins in my exposed forearms as she quickly ditched her friends. "Never thought I'd see you here."

"Why not?"

"Just seemed to me like you were more of the Midtown VIP social scene, not here." She invited herself to the seat next to mine, sliding down sensually. "Waiting for someone?"

"Not really," I spoke, dragging my pupils across her exposed skin. My incisors tingled at the thought of plummeting my canine teeth into her unblemished flesh, the mental picture of draining her body of her life fluid caused my lower region to respond positively. "Can I buy you a drink?"

"Apple martini," she expressed to the bartender, then turned her attention back to me. "I never noticed your accent until now. You're from the U.K.?"

"Nigeria. My ancestors are from Lagos." I nodded my appreciation at the bartender for giving me a refill as Cyndi sipped her drink. "What about you?"

"We're from Louisiana, down in the delta," she wiggled in her seat each time she took a sip, almost as if she was subconsciously begging me to drag my fingertip into the delta between her thighs. "My mama and pap both from Grand Isle, and I graduated from Tulane before moving here and interning for your company." Her exaggerated accent came along with a smile was as wide as the Mississippi, winking at me prior to downing the rest of her drink.

"What a coincidence. I lived in Louisiana for a while." I spoke, taking note at her perky breasts protruding from underneath her sheer blouse. "Nice place."

"Oh yea? When?"

1936, I mused to myself. "It was a while ago, plus I was further inland. So," I hurriedly changed the subject, "what you and your friends doing tonight?"

"Well, it is supposed to be a girl's night out, but I'm sure I can get rid of them for a little while. That is: if you got something else for me to do?" she squeezed her thighs together tightly, running her fingertips along my knee.

"I might have something for you," I openly leered at the same thing every other man in the bar was peeking at. "Get rid of

your friends." I checked my phone, paid my tab and made my way to the front of the club with her on my heels to my car. The perfect ending to a great day was about to be Cyndi and she didn't even know it.

"Vasilios, I gotta admit, I never thought you were into white women," she spoke timidly, lowering herself down into my Maserati while I held the door open for her. "But I should've known better, a man of your stature—"

"Be quiet." I hit the push-button start feeling the slight vibration from the engine as the car quietly came to life. I turned the jazz station up a little louder so she got the hint and headed to our destination. She wasn't my type, and it wasn't her skin tone either. As an immortal being, I'd tasted women in all flavors from all over the globe. No, she was a little too eager, too willing to be seen on my arm. Contrary to what others assumed of me, I preferred the chase. I like what I like, but I want to work for it. With Cyndi, it was being handed to me for the price of an apple martini.

Once we arrived at the hotel around the corner from the bar, she wasted no time stripping naked. I went to the bathroom to freshen up, came back and she was spread-eagled in the middle of the king-sized bed. "Like what you see?" she beckoned me over with a crooked index finger and a smile.

My eyes traveled the length of her neck first, taking note of the slight protrusion of the faded blue vein that meandered around to

the back of her head. "I got something to show you too," I spoke,
releasing the monster in my pants from my freshly pressed chinos.
"Like what you see?"

"Mmm...Vasilios I knew you were blessed," she mumbled,
scooting closer to the edge of the bed. With one move, she took me
inside her mouth devouring my shaft with long, smooth strokes of her
tongue. I rested my hand on top of her head and guided her on how
to pleasure me, smiling at her animalistic moans. The only pleasure
I would have is taking her life once this was all said and done.

We rolled around in the sheets for a while, and she did things
to me that helped to change my mind. When we parted ways a few
hours later, I decided I'd keep her around for a little while until I got
bored or until I found something else to do. She'd make little
comments here and there about us hooking up from time to time, but
I ignored her aspirations to be seen on my arm in a more public
setting. I knew I hadn't led her on to believe we'd done anything
more than hooking up one night, and certainly nothing that would
allude to her thinking we should move in together. How would that
look: me and my assistant living together? She still had to work,
after all, who would get my morning latte the way I liked it?

"Mr. Bello, there's someone here who says they have an
appointment with you but it's not on my schedule. Should I send
them away?" Cyndi's voice carried an indignant edge as it came
over the intercom on my desk.

"No, send her in," I knew she'd be upset but I didn't give a damn. *Maybe now she'll get the hint,* I thought as Kharynn's scent wafted through my door before she did. "Good afternoon, Kharynn. Nice to see you again."

Chapter 5

Kharynn

I stopped off at Starbucks and grabbed a cup of my favorite latte, then headed to the address on his business card. Even with a few hours of sleep, I was nervous; my stomach was twisted so tight I could hardly enjoy my latte. I tried calling everyone I knew to get my mind off my impromptu interview, but for some reason the only person available at 11 a.m. on a Monday was me. Finishing my venti latte with an extra shot of espresso to wake me up, I headed inside the building and signed in. After the security desk gave me a visitor's pass, I was pointed towards the elevators and told to have a great day.

As the elevator sped upwards towards the executive floors, I checked my face one more time against the elevator's blurry walls. I took a deep breath when it finally stopped and stepped directly into the executive offices for Bello Enterprises. I tried not to be impressed, but the further I walked inside, the harder it was. His offices were nothing like the standard office buildings I'd been in; the layout was reminiscent of a three-bedroom apartment with interior glass walls and plush carpeting. If all else failed, Vasilios could give me a job as a janitor; I wouldn't mind cleaning this space while catching up on my shows on the 80-inch flat-screen on the wall.

"Yes, can I help you?" the woman behind the desk rolled her eyes in my direction as if she could care less.

"I have a 1 o'clock with Bello." The latte had to have boosted my confidence somewhere between the elevator and the secretary's desk. "Let him know Kharynn Lewis is here."

"Lewis...Lewis...I'm not seeing your name on his calendar for today," she pounded the MacBook keys desperately to find my name.

"Just..." I fanned my hand at her sour expression. "...let him know I'm here." I dug in my purse as a distraction because I already felt the irritation creeping up my neck.

"Miss, I'm telling you that you aren't..."

"You know what? I'll go. But I'll also let Vasilios know he needs to do something about the level of incompetence in this office, it's overwhelming." I flung a handful of words laced with irritation in her direction, collecting the portfolio with my resume from the chair next to me.

"Wait, I'll..." she tapped the keys a few seconds longer then turned her attention to me, "Have a seat, I'll let him know you're here. We had the techs working on the server earlier and they may have deleted something in the interim."

I refused to sit for a second time, so I stood tapping my foot impatiently against the plush multicolored carpeting, fighting the urge to take my shoes off and wiggle my toes between the loops. I wasn't sure who hired this woman, but if I was going to be working here in any capacity, she needed to not be. *The server did it, huh. Girl bye,* I mumbled under my breath.

She waved me in the door behind her desk, and I brushed past her, adjusting my mood as I stepped inside of his corner office. Blinded by the sunlight pouring in from the floor to ceiling windows, I blinked for a few seconds to adjust my vision when I heard his voice.

"Good afternoon Vasilios. Thanks for seeing me on such short notice," I smiled politely.

"Have a seat," he spoke invitingly enough. "Now, have you thought about what you want to do here?"

"You know it doesn't matter; I'd be ok with cleaning this office if that was all you had."

"Mmm, can't wait to get that ass bent over the desk..." I thought I heard Vasilios mumble to himself.

"Excuse me?"

"I'm sorry, I was thinking about a business matter," he cleared his throat and adjusted his tie. "Now what were we discussing?"

"The job?"

"Yes, yes…the job." He fumbled around for a few minutes, shuffling paperwork back and forth on his desk. "How much do you know about Microsoft Excel, PowerPoint, and Outlook?"

"I'm well versed in the complete Microsoft Office suite of workplace programs," I boasted proudly. "I'm also proficient in PeopleSoft, Kenexa, ADP payroll, I type 75 words per minute, and I have an excellent memory."

"Impressive background," he nodded, impressed with my skill set. "You learned all that at Southwest?"

"No, I worked for a dentist in Alpharetta for a while in college. Learned a lot, but my days were repetitive. Patients, paperwork, vendor reps…after a while it became monotonous."

"How would you like to be my secretary?" he toyed lackadaisically with an expensive pen, while his seductive brown eyes remained fixated on my cleavage.

I tried to hide my excitement, considering I was semi unemployed a few hours ago. "I wouldn't mind at all. How much does the position pay?"

"I'll see to it that you're adequately compensated." And with that, I had a better job than the one I was contemplating leaving. "Have dinner with me tonight. We can celebrate your new position here at Bello Enterprises."

"I…uhmm…I don't think that's appropriate. But thank you."

"Hmmm," he growled lowly; the sparkle in his eyes spelled the kind of trouble that was sure to have me melted in a puddle of crazy once it was all said and done. His penetrating gaze held my face for a second before he turned away disappointed. "Well, Cyndi will get the paperwork you're going to need for human resources. Make sure you leave everything with her, Trina will kill me if I told you to start tomorrow and we find out you spent time in prison for embezzlement," he joked. "As soon as I have the green light from them, I'll give you a call. Any questions?"

"Nope. I'll just wait for your call then." I pressed a tight-lipped smile in his direction, and he returned the same. "So, you said Cyndi has the paperwork?"

"Yes." He pressed a button and spoke to the intercom on his desk. "Cyndi bring me a new hire packet."

Vasilios and I were making small talk when the door opened. I could tell from her walk Cyndi was pissed. One minute I'd represented myself as one of Vasilios's peers and the next she was bringing me an orientation packet. "Welcome to Bello Enterprises," she uttered, uninterested in my response. "What branch of the business will you be based out of?"

"I'll be based out of this office," I knew my next words would get her attention. I'd only been in this woman's space for a few minutes and she'd already gotten under my skin. "Vasilios hired me as his secretary."

"EXCUSE ME?" her head rocked back and forth between me and Vasilios in bewilderment, but her icy glare was reserved for my new boss. "What does she mean she's your secretary? Is this your way of telling me I'm fired?" she raged.

"Cyndi—"

"Wait," she tossed the packet on his desk and clasped her hands together with a smile. "Wait…does this mean what I think it does?" she squealed with delight.

"Depends." Vasilios watched her with a raised eyebrow while tugging on his beard. "What do you think it means?"

"Oh, baby…" she walked around the desk with her arms stretched open. "Baby, finally we're…you were going to surprise me…I love it! I LOVE IT!"

"Yea, I was gonna surprise you alright," he stood up from his chair only to take a seat on the edge of his desk. "You're moving down the hall to work for Owen McDonald."

"Work? What…wait…I'll be working for Owen?"

"Surprise." His smile didn't hold the slightest bit of humor as Cyndi covered the lower half of her face with her hands.

"Vasilios, you can't…" she stood shakily for a second before marching closer to his desk where he sat unbothered. "Why—"

"Strike two, Cyndi. If you insist on referring to me by my first name, you can do so from the sidewalk. As long as the plaque on the outside of this building says Bello Enterprises, as in Vasilios Bello Enterprises, you will respect my wishes. Owen is waiting for you." he abruptly dismissed her. "Trina, can you come into my office and take care of the paperwork for our new hire?" he barked into the speaker on his desk.

"Is this what a day at the office normally looks like?" I chuckled in my palm at his frustrated glare, trying to lighten the mood. Whether he was tossing around criminals in the middle of the night or reassigning inept employees, Vasilios was still a handsome man.

"My apologies that you had to witness such unpleasantness," his voice dropped to his normal timbre. "I run a tight ship, but I'm also an affable man. Sometimes the staff tends to take advantage of that."

"Oh, no problem. I just wanted to make sure we were on the page," I retracted. "Just so I know what I'm getting myself into."

"If there's one thing I can guarantee Kharynn: working at Bello Enterprises will be nothing like anything you've done before," he reassured me. "This is going to be the best job you've ever had in your entire life."

I hoped he was right. "Looking forward to it."

Vasilios

Her scent alone was enough to rouse my senses to dizzying heights; the sandalwood and freesia body mist sprayed lightly across her skin complimented her natural scent perfectly. Her lips were moving but I vaguely heard her words. I was more focused on the pout in her lips; both plump and succulent…I wanted to drag my tongue across her second fleshiest attribute. Kharynn's natural perfume between her smooth thighs was subtle yet obvious to all five of my senses. I wanted this woman in a way that she couldn't have possibly experienced in her lifetime.

"Anything else, Mr. Bello?" Trina's voice brought me out of my reverie of the woman who left my office a few minutes ago.

"No, that'll be all." I dismissed the head of human resources more of an afterthought, my mind stuck on Kharynn. "Wait a second, Trina." I stopped her as she prepared to go back to her office. "If you can put a rush on that paperwork; off the record, Ms. Lewis did share that she's looking for something soon as possible and I don't want the competition to potentially get a leg up on us with this one."

"Will do, Bello. My office will get right on it," Trina drifted out as quietly as she'd come in, leaving me alone with my musings once more.

I closed my eyes and envisioned she was here once again in my presence, minus the peach-colored dress topped with a white blazer that she wore to her interview. Instead, my mind's greedy eye replaced her attire with a white lace bra and panty set; I was in awe of her semi-nude frame. Crystal embellished Louboutin heels adorned her dainty feet as she strode confidently from the door to my desk. With her glossed lips slightly parted, she sat atop the mahogany wood facing me, running her small hands down my broad chest. Kharynn wrapped my tie up in her little fist, gently pulling me towards her she pressed her lips atop my own, slipping her tongue between my flesh...

"Mr. Bello, we're almost done with the meeting," a voice crackled from the intercom on my desk. "Is there anything you wanted to add?"

Switching back to reality, I was relieved that I was in my office alone, the stiffness of my manhood would've been unprofessional under any other circumstances. "I trust that you were impeccable in my absence, Gary. Thank the team for a great year." I replied, adjusting myself to relieve the mounting pressure.

"Will do."

Kharynn had my mind, body, and quite possibly soul already and she didn't know it. Soon...very soon there wouldn't be a doubt in her mind.

*

After I cleared her from my thoughts, I took a few more calls before leaving the office for the day. Unlike most men in my position, I preferred to get out and about, touching every aspect of the company with my own two hands. I wasn't going to grab a hammer on a job site, hop behind the counter at any of my five-star restaurants, or be the substitute cameraman at any of my studios, but I did visit to make sure everyone was on the up and up.

I walked across the parking garage with my key fob in hand and blazer tossed across my forearm. My senses tingled with anticipation of a potential kill at the sound of dainty footfalls attempt to creep up behind me. Once I reached my car, I pretended to fumble with the fob as the steps became closer and closer, ducking near a truck on my right side. Tapping the button to open the door, I slid my jacket in the passenger seat and loosened my tie further. "Cyndi, what do you want?" I called out to the open air, listening to my voice echo back to me from the concrete walls.

"So, who is she?" Cyndi strode from behind the bumper of the Jeep Cherokee, arms folded across her chest.

"Pardon me?"

"The woman who you pushed me out of a position that I've held since you moved Bello Enterprises into this building. Who is she, Vasilios?"

"Cyndi go back to work." I lowered myself down into the car and hit the push-button start, then turned the air conditioning down a few notches.

"No, Vasilios, I think I should know," she reached out to stop me from closing the door in her face. "I thought we were building something here—"

"You couldn't have thought that." I chuckled, relaxing in the plush seat. "I don't live Atlanta, have no interest in living in Atlanta, and you've never been invited to come where I am. Building what?"

We got into a brief staring match that I wasn't backing down from. Cyndi finally broke our gaze with a slow blink and fake smile across her face. "Vasilios, you don't mean that. You can't. Remember you told me you could see yourself falling for me that night?"

Now that was a possibility; I would've said anything to get her to wrap her lips around my manhood one more time before we parted ways. Cyndi had a talent that was being underutilized as my secretary. "I was drunk."

She stared at me incredulously for a few more seconds hoping I'd give in, but I refused. "You don't mean that. I'll give you some time because I know you don't mean that. When you come to your senses, you know where to find me, right?"

"Yea, down the hall at Owen's. Now if you're done…"

"I love you Vasilios," she released her grip on the car's door to make a pointless attempt to lean in. I took that as an opportunity to close the door in her face. Checking the rear-view camera in case she was trying to fake an injury, I backed out of my parking spot and sped out the lot. This woman was delusional, but she was harmless compared to me.

After making a few turns, I ended up on I-85 south headed to East Point. I had a construction site not too far from Tyler Perry's new studios; with him deciding to revitalize that area, franchisees were scrambling to buy up the land and take advantage of potential celebrity clients. We were awarded the contract for a strip mall with a Starbucks in the parking lot, and judging from the progress made, we were on track to finish ahead of time, earning an additional 4 million dollars in bonus. Bello Enterprises was the most trusted name in building, and I was proud of my accomplishments in this lifetime.

As I toured the job site, my mind was drawn back to the chocolate beauty who held my heart. I couldn't believe she turned me…ME down for a dinner date. As much time as I'd spent implanting suggestions into her mind, I needed to stop to find out what she liked. I needed to be the object of her affection; in time she would crave my attention as much as I looked forward to feeding on hers.

I trotted back to my vehicle scrolling through my recent calls. Once I found who I was looking for, I hit talk on her phone number. "Hello?"

"Hi, Kharynn?"

"Speaking. Wait…Vasilios?"

"How are you?" Once I heard her light alto coming through my car's speakers, my day was instantly brighter.

"I'm great, thanks to you. I can't express my gratitude for you giving me a chance, considering you just met me last night."

"Not a problem, like I said earlier, I've seen you in action," I smirked, merging onto I-75 north. "By the way, I wasn't trying to make you feel uncomfortable earlier—"

"Why would you think I was uncomfortable?"

"About the dinner comment. You—"

"I didn't want to say yes while we were in your office, anyone could have been listening on that little intercom on your desk. The last thing I need is for anyone to assume any impropriety concerning my position with the company, especially your former secretary," she giggled.

"So, you will have dinner with me?"

"Of course. Name the restaurant and I'll meet you there."

I planned to bring her to my home, but a restaurant would do for now. "Ray's in Alpharetta at 8?"

"Got it on my calendar," she replied over the scribbling noise in the background. "I'll see you there."

"I'll pick you up."

"Vasilios, I can—"

"Kharynn, don't insult me. Text me your address."

"Oh, ok. I'll see you at 7 then?"

"7 it is."

"Bye Vasilios," I heard the smile in her voice before she hung up.

I smiled to myself with the knowledge that she was anxiously anticipating our dinner date. If I played my cards right, and I usually did, this would be the beginning of a love affair that would span over an eternity.

Chapter 6

Kharynn

I was on cloud nine heading back to Chamblee from Bello Enterprises, even the beginning of afternoon traffic didn't bother me. Vasilios not only created a position for me with his company, but he'd also paid me my monthly salary at Southwest before taxes as my weekly take home pay. Depending on how things went over these next six weeks, it might be safe to say I would be handing in my resignation at the airline soon.

My phone ringing through the car's speakers demanded my attention for the time being; one glance at the screen on the car's console, I saw it was Maxine. "Did you call Bello Enterprises yet?" I rushed, not bothering to say hello.

"That's what I was calling to tell you. Girl, I got an interview tomorrow at 11 o'clock for cafeteria manager!" she squealed.

"Manager? Girl, I'm so happy for you!" I cried. "Bout time somebody recognized you for your skill!"

"I know!" she exhaled. "Leave it up to these yellow letters and I'd probably be the night supervisor for the rest of my life! At least manager would look better on my resume if this doesn't work out."

"Who are you scheduled to interview with?"

"I left a message on Bello's number this morning and somebody named Trina called me back a few minutes ago."

"Trina? Girl, you got the job, she's the head of HR," I shared. "Now if it was that damn Cyndi…"

"How you know these people? Girl…"

"Yes, I talked to Bello today too. He made me his secretary," I gloated.

"His secretary?" she snickered. "Oh, so you gonna be working right up under him, huh." We both busted out laughing at her double meaning.

"Not what I applied for, but I guess so." I dabbed the corners of my eyes from laughing at her crazy self. "I was looking for something temporary until Southwest called me back and that's what he offered."

"Until they call you back? Girl, what happened at that place now?"

We gossiped about the job until I pulled into the parking garage at my apartment building. Maxine didn't know about me and Charles, nobody knew for that matter, so I couldn't tell her my gut feeling that stuck with me from the moment the union rep called and laid me off over the phone. Had it not been for Bello, I didn't know what my fate would be but thank God we crossed paths.

"Let me get off this phone, I gotta get this house cleaned up before tonight…"

"Tonight? What's happening tonight?"

"Well, Bello taking me out to celebrate…"

"Ahhhh…ahkay boss lady," she snickered slyly. "Y'all celebrating today, tomorrow y'all gonna be…"

"Girl, stop. He just being nice." I felt an inner glow knowing that a billionaire was interested in taking little ol' me out.

"Well, I'll be looking forward to my dinner date tomorrow then, since Mr. Bello is so generous," Maxine spoke haughtily then busted out laughing again. "I'm happy for you though. I mean getting paid to see the world is ok and all, but I know it gets lonely on those international flights seeing some of the most beautiful places on the planet and not having someone who loves you by your side to enjoy the view with."

"That's the last thing I'm thinking about at work." I lied.

"If it was me, I'd be sneaking me a little somebody in the cargo area to work that thang out," she cackled, her dirty mind wrapping up our conversation. "Lemme let you go, I'll call you tomorrow and let you know how it went. Talk to you later girl!"

"I'm praying for you hun!" I called out, disconnecting the call. My exit was coming up, so I came off I-285 at Chamblee-

Dunwoody. While I sat at the stoplight, I thought about Maxine's words.

I did want someone who loved me by my side as I flew to Aruba, Cabo San Lucas, Turks and Caicos, and Montego Bay for work. Even when me and Charles went to Santorini, Lisbon, Madrid, Rio, Milan…all that was with the unspoken understanding that he belonged to someone else. We'd go sightseeing, shopping, exploring…do all the things tourists did. I'd made love to someone else's husband on at least three continents.

But at the end of the day, he was never truly mine. I thought that was what I wanted, but as the days turned into weeks, the weeks turned into months, and the months turned into years, I realized that he was going home to someone who made sure he was taken care of. Someone who, no matter what he'd moaned to me in the heat of passion, Charles went home to someone who loved him unconditionally in spite of his trespasses against her. Charles went home to love, peace, compromise. Charles went home to a family, to a love that was pure from his twin daughters, regardless of what he and his wife went through. And me…I came home to nothing. An empty bed and a head full of memories, regrets, and what-ifs.

The light changed to green and my car took off down the street. Three minutes later I pulled into my complex with a heavy heart and an even heavier soul. I trudged up the steps cussing myself out for being so naïve. I hated that mentally my happiness was always overshadowed by HIM. Every time something good happened in my life my mind would automatically switch to him. What he would think. What he would say. How he would react. An argument we had six months ago. How he touched my body in ways that had me screaming his name. Always Charles.

Remorse met me at my front door; once inside I peeled off my interview clothes and sat in the middle of my closet, not knowing where to go from here. Charles and I were done, and I could file the memories of our escapades away in the back of my mind as I looked forward to the future. Vasilios Bello, the richest man in Atlanta, invited me to dinner and I had to be on my best behavior, even though I wanted him in a whole other way.

Vasilios

After I made sure Trina set Maxine up with the kitchen manager interview that she would be hired into, I left. I had to make sure I was ready for my date with the woman I couldn't get out of my head, the woman who would birth my babies, the woman who stole my heart and had no clue. Kharynn thought we had reservations for Ray's this evening, but I had other plans. Me taking her somewhere in Atlanta was too easy, too predictable, and one thing I wasn't was average. No, I had to show her who I was and what she'd have to look forward to with me as an integral part of her life.

"Siri, call Tony," I called out to the car's interior on my short ride home. Here in the city, I had a condo in north Buckhead not too far from Sandy Springs that overlooked GA-400 near the king and queen towers. Traffic was a nightmare, but I knew shortcuts that no one else knew of.

"Calling Tony." Waiting for the call to connect, I debated whether to take her to Spago or to the best Thai food in L.A., which just so happened to be a food truck. "Aye Tony, Bello. Jet good?"

"Yea, we thought it was gonna be a major repair, but found out it wasn't. You need a ride?"

"Yea, I got reservations in L.A. tonight." I fiddled with the gear shift as I spoke. Kharynn already had me nervous, but in a good way.

"I got you, boss. Need anything for the flight?"

"Five dozen roses, a bottle of champagne and a box of Belgian chocolate should do it."

"Gotcha. Glad to see you getting back out there, boss."

"Yea, me too. Thanks, man." I hung up smirking to myself.

Tony was an older gentleman, by modern-day standards, whose beliefs were similar to mine: we both still believed in that old-fashioned kind of love. That kind of love where the man courted his woman the same way his father courted his mother to solidify that forever type of love that stood the test of time no matter what. Kharynn was that for me.

After maneuvering down a few side streets, I pulled into my parking spot at one of Atlanta's most exclusive addresses. My private entrance was well hidden behind frosted glass doors, allowing for a discreet entrance inside my 2,000 square foot one-bedroom condo. Kharynn was gonna love this once I convinced her to let her guard down, a few more late-night visits should get her where I wanted her to be. Searching through my expansive collection of high-end suits, something from my past crept into my memory to be recalled for this moment:

The year was 1949. I was staying with an older lady who rented out the rooms in her home after her husband died. I found her in the Negro Motorist Green Book given to me before I left Mississippi; no one I knew was aware of my life as an immortal being. I'm sure she only wanted to be sure I was safe as I traveled, considering I was a black man in the south.

Seeing that the widow needed the help, sometimes I'd fix stuff around the house, other times I'd help with the groceries when she was a little short. She encouraged me to go into town to meet a nice young lady, but that wasn't what brought me to the area. One hot boring Sunday, I gave in and went to the rundown wooden structure they were calling the house of the Lord and met someone.

Ever since the day Sarah and I met at church, she'd been discreetly following me all over town. There were times when I'd be in my rented room reading and I'd catch her peeking through the corner of the cutout that could be interpreted as a window. Or I would go to town for a shave and a haircut and she'd conveniently bring her oldest son in the shop, pretending as if our meetings were by accident. She'd strike up a random conversation for five minutes, then go about her way. Nothing that had to do with any one subject in particular; it was usually about working in the fields, fishing, or something about how her children were suffering because her no good husband ran off to God knows where. She and I didn't have a deep connection in my opinion, as a matter of fact, we were far from it. I knew she wanted more, yet the more she pursued me the less interested I was.

Purely by accident, we ended up at a juke joint deep down in the bayou one warm country night listening to a kid who called himself Muddy Waters strumming on a guitar and playing a

harmonica singing blues music. Making my way through the packed
crowd of sweaty bodies winding back and forth to the lone melody, I
made my way to the bar and, after a few minutes, flagged down the
bartender. "Aye, lemme get anotha shotta that moonshine!" I yelled
over the harmonica whining melodically through the rickety shack.

"Is that...awww, yea baby! Look who hea'!" a voice yelled
from behind me before she appeared, pressing and winding her hips
against my manhood. "I knew I was wearing you down! Come on
home to mama!"

"Whoa, whoa, whoa...slow down woman!" I yelled playfully,
wrapping my arms around her waist. "We got all night."

Normally I didn't take advantage of women, but normal went
out the window an hour and two jars of moonshine ago. The more
Muddy strummed that guitar and belted out those notes, the hotter it
got in that shack and the more emboldened the women became. Out
of nowhere, Sarah propped a leg up on my upper thigh and popped
that coochie on my chest so hard I had no other choice but to take
her outside on the side of that shack and cool that pussy off.

I picked her up and hurried towards the exit. As we rushed
between the bodies, I caught the eye of one of her neighbors
eyeballing me like I was the last chicken wing at Sunday dinner.
Nodding sideways to signal that she should follow us outside, I
pushed Sarah out first and trudged around the back of the structure,

watching her clothes trail along behind her as she walked. "Vasilios, I knew you wanted to fuck me. I knew it," she slurred.

"Me too," her neighbor purred as she rounded the corner. "We gonna have some fun tonight."

"Jean what you doing—"

"Shhh…she just gonna pick up where you leave off, that's all," I encouraged, slowly yet gently helping her down to her knees. "You don't wanna have no fun?"

"Yea…" she was face to face with my stiff member. "If we do this, I don't want you to think I'm a bad person, Vasilios. I'm a good woman. I take good care of my chirren and go to church ev'ry Sunday…"

"Mmhmm…" I moaned, kissing her friend on the lips as she took my little head in her mouth…

"Man, this crazy life," I had to chuckle at myself, remembering the surprised look on Jean's face when I sunk my teeth into her neck after I left Sarah's body floating in the bayou as food for my reptilian brothers. Both women wanted me to themselves and tried to outdo each other in their efforts to please me. What they both failed to understand was that I had no interest in being the object of either woman's affections. Residents of the small town in Louisiana not too far from the banks of the Mississippi River knew me as the nice, quiet man who stayed out of the way and kept to myself. I loved women, the female form excited me with all of its soft curves and smooth folds, wet places and moans, thick thighs and throaty sighs that I would become lost in while she gripped the back of my head and euphorically wheezed my name.

Kharynn didn't deserve that version of me, she deserved the potential mate that she would mesh with. She deserved the version of me that was the opposite of what she was accustomed to. She deserved the best version of me that I could give. And tonight, that's who she would get.

*

She texted me her address an hour ago, so currently I was sitting outside Kharynn's apartment building waiting for her to come downstairs. My damp palms patted nervously against the woodgrain steering wheel on my Bentley. I texted her to let her know where I was parked just as she stepped out of the building. Her strapless all white maxi dress billowed in the breeze, the wisps of hair at the nape of her neck gently kissed her brunette tinted skin. Her smile was genuine once she spotted me sitting in the car admiring her silhouette that I could clearly see as the wind pressed the translucent material against her frame.

I stepped out of the car to open her door as she pranced towards me, my beautiful fantasy in the flesh. Sooner rather than later she would belong to me. "Hey, Bello. Been a while since somebody took me out for a meal."

"I don't see why not. You're gorgeous, if you were mine, I'd show you off every chance I got." I helped her and her dress in and closed the door. Jogging around to the other side of the vehicle I hopped inside and took advantage of the opportunity to take in her beauty for a while longer.

"Well, thank you, but…" she began, then stopped. I followed her eyes to see a man peering through my front window as if he was trying to see who was inside. "I can't believe this."

"What's wrong, love?" I willed myself to not stroke that spot on the back of her neck that had been calling my name for as long as I'd known her.

"That's my ex." Her expression changed as she reached for the door handle. "Vasilios can you give me a few minutes, I need to…"

I grabbed her hand and gently placed it back in her lap. "Eat. You need to eat, and I need to feed you." I started up the car and put it in reverse. Charles seemed like a reasonable man, but if he was going through these lengths for a woman currently sitting in another man's car, he was the fool for letting her slip through his fingers in the first place.

"But…"

"But we're going to be late." I shifted the car into drive and drove past her ex standing on the sidewalk looking lost. "Buckle up."

"I—ok." I loved a woman who followed my direction without an argument. "We're going to be early for our…wait. Shouldn't we be going north?"

"Yea, if we were going to Ray's we would be. But since we're on our way to the airport…"

"The airport?"

"Yea, Peachtree-DeKalb is right around the corner."

"Peachtree-Dekalb? We're not going to Hartsfield-Jackson? Now I'm really confused," she mused softly to the window.

"Yea, my private jet is parked there for now. Have you ever been to Spago in—"

"L.A.? We're going to L.A.?" she squealed excitedly, dancing in her seat.

"So, you've been?"

"No, I always wanted to go, but—" she stopped short, knowing not to say his name in my presence. For that, I was grateful. Grateful that I didn't have to kill his ass tonight for depriving this beautiful woman of a five-star meal when she deserved that and more. Much, much more.

"You're going to love it," I continued, breaking the awkward silence before it became a problem and ruined our dinner date. "You've never had Wagyu like they serve it."

"So lemme get this straight: we're getting on a plane and flying to L.A. so I can try this steak?"

"Can you think of another reason why we shouldn't?"

"I thought we were going to Ray's," she smiled and fanned herself as we rode down Peachtree. "Spago is ok I guess."

"Ok, huh." I reached over and patted her knee. "Can I ask you a question?"

"Sure."

"How do you feel about chocolate?"

"Oh, one of the ultimate aphrodisiacs. I love chocolate."

"What do you know about chocolate being an aphrodisiac?" I raised an eyebrow while pulling into my parking space at the airport.

"Tryptophan releases serotonin, which is the chemical in the brain that regulates arousal and phenylethylamine tells me that I'm in love. But that's according to scientific research."

I stepped out of the driver's seat and jogged to the passenger side to open her door. "Ahhh, I got a scientist working for me, I see. Tell me this, my little genius: what do you think?"

"I think that if I wanted to fall in love, a Hershey bar wouldn't have anything to do with it." She stepped out of the car and did a little twirl before switching her thick hips towards the entrance. God damn this woman was sexy. "Love…true love has a way of pursuing two people until it tackles them both and forces them to relent."

"Tackles them down?" I chuckled, still resisting my urges to touch her skin. The light scent of jasmine and blackberries followed her as she moved freely through the airport. "You looking forward to being raped by love?"

"If that's what it takes for me to have it." She held her hand out behind her and I took it, pulling me closer to her as if we were lovers and not what we were. "You wouldn't want love to be that shining bright light that gave you a reason to come home?"

"Shining light, yea. Emotional rape, nah, you can have that." I chuckled, leading her to the tarmac. "This is us, you ready?"

"Ready as I'll ever be. Let's go." She climbed the narrow steps with an enthusiasm that I hadn't expected but was a pleasant surprise.

On this trip, she'd know my true intentions for her. She'd know that I was her quarterback in this game of love, she'd know that I was the only player on the field for the game of winning her heart. This Charles person was whack if he couldn't even treat her to a night at Spago, I had to find out what else he'd deprived her of and make her dreams come true. I loved this woman. I'd wait for as long as it took, but she'd see that I was the only thing she needed in this lifetime.

Chapter 7

Kharynn

It had been a few weeks since I got the job at Bello Enterprises, and I couldn't be happier. A month ago, if anyone would've told me that I'd be working anywhere other than Southwest Airlines I probably would've called them crazy. The people I worked with were helpful and understood that I was acclimating to my new position. When I had questions that required me to talk to Cyndi, Trina, the head of HR, would have that conversation with her.

Vasilios went back to Raleigh a few days after he flew me to L.A. for dinner in the most perfect way, but I didn't mind because we still saw one another on FaceTime every night. We'd go for ice cream on Sundays before he dropped off at home, and I loved walking through Brookhaven holding hands and sharing a cone with him. He'd send me links to songs that were playing on the radio as we rode to Spago, bringing up all the beautiful memories I had of our first date. He listened when I spoke and didn't change the conversation to something about him. Or his wife. Or his kids. Bello was so much more than an executive at the company I worked for, and to him, I was more than another nameless face. To me, he was a real friend.

At first, I thought he was a pompous ass, judging by the way he handled Cyndi during my interview. Still, I gave him a chance to show me a different side of himself. We had a great time that evening, and the next day I found myself back in Georgia on a boat at Lake Allatoona on a champagne cruise with him and a few of the vice presidents at Bello Enterprises. I was introduced as his secretary; however, his colleagues were there with their wives. At that moment, I knew Mr. Bello had other intentions with me, and a part of me was ready for whatever our future held.

My voice mail ringer had been vibrating in my purse for the past fifteen minutes while I finished up a memo from Vasilios that needed to go out to the company. After hitting send, I grabbed my phone and hit the voicemail button.

Good morning Ms. Lewis, this is Mr. Farr your union rep at Southwest. I have some important information to discuss with you, please give me a call today at 404-555-9574. Looking forward to hearing from you.

"Hope he doesn't think I'm coming in to cover anyone's shift," I mumbled under my breath. After doing a little investigating on my own, I found out I was the only person in the company currently on furlough, not to mention Southwest Airlines was still hiring for my position. I called the human resources department who told me their hands were tied; any grievances I had would have to go through my union rep who would then bring the information to them. When I asked who I should call if I had a problem with my union rep, I was given the runaround. Either way, I didn't care; I got that 'odd job' Mr. Farr suggested that was covering my bills so anything else was irrelevant.

"Hey Trina, I'm going to step out for a few minutes to return an important call, is that ok?" On the days Vasilios wasn't in the office I wasn't required to report to anyone, but I didn't want to be rude and walk away from my desk.

"Sure, you're fine," she muted her conference call, waving me off. I locked my desk, grabbed my purse, and headed downstairs to return the call from my main job.

"Hey, Mr. Farr?"

"Yes, Farr speaking."

"I'm returning your call from earlier, this is Kharynn Lewis," I huffed. I wasn't faking professional courtesy with him; he'd decided to furlough me on a whim, not caring if I sunk or swam. I couldn't prove Charles was behind my current leave or not, and this was the only person who would…or wouldn't…give me an idea of whether or not I was right.

"Yes Kharynn, I was giving you a call to let you know that your flight privileges have been restored. We expect to see you on Flight 3026 from Atlanta to Los Angeles on the 5th. Will that be a problem?"

"The 5th of next month?" I fidgeted with my lip gloss, spreading a second coat on my lips to replace the one I'd practically licked off from earlier. "That's in another two weeks. Are there any flight crews I can fly with anytime during this pay period?"

"Unfortunately, all of our flight crews are full, especially after we ramped up spring staffing," he let slip from his lips. I don't think he even realized his mistake; he was talking so fast. "I'm calling in a favor even getting you on this flight."

"Who's the pilot?"

"Excuse me?"

"I'd like to know who the pilot is on Flight 3026 from Atlanta to Los Angeles on the 5th please."

"Uhmm…" I heard paperwork shuffling in the background before he came back on the line, "Whitlow. Charles Whitlow."

"Oh."

"Have you filed a grievance against Mr. Whitlow? If so, I'd have to have you—"

"No, it's fine." I rolled my eyes to the heavens and shook my head. "It's fine. I'll be there."

"Alright Ms. Lewis, if you don't have any further questions—"

"Actually, I do. Why was I the only flight attendant in the company furloughed because of budget cuts, yet the company has over 200 new members of the flight crew who were all brought in after I was placed on leave?"

"Uhmm…" Mr. Farr cleared his throat, his self-assured demeanor from a few seconds ago gone. "The company made the decision…"

"Not from what I gathered in speaking with the head of human resources a few weeks ago. You know, next time you and your friend decide to deprive someone of their livelihood, please make sure they don't know their rights. Do me a favor: let someone in human resources know the company will be hearing from my lawyer once I send him this recorded phone call." I ended our conversation so he couldn't get another word in.

Once Vasilios found out I'd been 'furloughed', he contacted his friend, who happened to be the VP of HR and Chief People Officer of the company. Jan was unaware of any lay-offs, and as far as she was concerned, she would have known first. Upon a little further investigation, they found the relationship between Charles and Mr. Farr. Apparently, in exchange for preferential treatment on his flights, John would handle his 'mishaps' with the flight attendants. I wasn't the first person my union rep made the sole decision to lay off because his friend was mad, and his entire family had been comped on flights to every city Southwest had a hub. This whole operation was bigger than me, but I was the only one who had the courage to fight back. Neither John nor Charles had been walked out of Southwest…yet.

I dropped my phone inside my bag and took a minute to feel the warm Georgia sun beam on my face, brightening my day with its rays. Jan gave me the option to come back to Southwest when we first spoke, but I declined. Bello Enterprises was paying me triple my salary at the airlines for half of the work, not to mention I'd be at home on the weekends. True, I had to deal with Atlanta traffic, but that was a small price to pay for my sanity.

I debated on whether I wanted to go back to work for the day, or call Vasilios and take the rest of the day off. With it being Friday, my work for the week was already done. If anything, I'd be taunted by Cyndi for the rest of the afternoon. The executives normally worked a half-day, getting their weekends started early, but we executive assistants were left to answer calls and send emails for the latter half of our day. I'm sure my boss wouldn't mind; he'd been trying to charter me a flight for the past few days. Our office was small, and I didn't need word getting out that me and Mr. Bello had something going on, hence the reason I was able to come and go as I pleased.

As my heels clacked against the marble floor in the building's entryway, I fished my phone from the bottom of my bag for the second time in five minutes. *Who could be calling me on a Friday morning?* "Hello?"

"I was calling to see if you were done playing games," Charles's voice growled in my ear. "Tell that boyfriend of yours I'm back."

"Oh, you back, huh." I pushed the button for the elevator and tapped my foot against the marble floor as I waited.

"Yea I'm back, dammit! I got you your job back, didn't I?"

"How did you know I wasn't working, Charles?" I stepped inside the elevator.

"Does it matter? I'm not gonna keep playing with you, Kharynn! Be ready when I come over tonight, damn!" he spat before he hung up.

"Sure Charles, I'll be ready," I mumbled to myself, glad I was on the elevator alone. I guess he forgot he 'broke up' with me, not the other way around. These past few weeks with Vasilios let me know exactly what I was missing wasting my time with Charles Whitlow. Between the phone calls to check on my well-being, the weekend visits, and the late-night 'Facetime and chill' sessions, I'd forgotten all about what's-his-face at the airlines. I felt alive, I felt free, I felt…I felt something I'd never felt from a man, not even my father. I felt safe.

By the time I reached my floor, my phone rang for the third time. Reaching in my bag as the doors slid open, I didn't bother to check the screen first before answering. If it was Charles, I'd remind him of his words a few weeks ago. "Yes."

"Come see me today."

"You must be a mind reader, I was thinking that same thing," I cheesed, watching Cyndi saunter away from my desk looking suspicious. "You know I'm still at work."

"Leave. I'm at the airport right now, do I need to send a car for you too?" he snickered playfully.

"Let Trina know you gave the ok," I hit the button on the elevator to go back downstairs. "Traffic isn't bad right now, so—"

"I just put a file on your desk that needs your immediate attention," Cyndi's voice soured behind me. "As an executive secretary, it's your responsibility to act immediately on any files given to you by the executive team, and that's straight from Owen's desk."

"Tell her to go to hell. Owen isn't even in the office," Vasilios gritted

. "How does she have anything that needs your immediate attention unless it's something she didn't do herself yesterday?"

"I'll take care of it after lunch, Cyndi." I dismissed her as an afterthought watching the elevator doors as they slid open.

"You take a lunch? Hmph…" she walked back to her side of the office with a smug expression. "I bring my lunch; you can tell which one of us knows what they are doing and which one of us doesn't." I heard her voice until the doors closed.

"Vasilios—"

"Don't let her rattle you like that; she's trying to break you. I have the final say on what needs your attention and what doesn't; you don't work for her."

"Why does she do that though?"

"I don't know."

"If I didn't know any better, I'd think the two of you had something going on. Do you?" I waited for an answer. I knew how these workplace romances went and didn't want to be a part of a love triangle between my boss and his ex-secretary.

"We're not dating, Kharynn. We've never dated, I give you my word."

"But that day in your office she said—"

"Do you trust me, Kharynn?"

"Yes." I wasn't sure why, I just did. Someone who made me feel the things he did, someone like him couldn't possibly be lying to me. He had no reason to do so, what would he gain from that?

"From now until Monday morning, let's not talk about anything work-related, ok?"

"Ok." No matter what, Vasilios always managed to put a smile on my face regardless of my mood. "What are we doing this weekend?" I changed the subject.

"I might have a surprise for you," he mumbled sexily. "But only if you're up to it."

"If I'm up to it? What are you up to this time?"

"Nothing, Mrs. ...I mean Ms. Lewis," he chuckled in my ear. "You know, the quicker you get here, the quicker I can satisfy your...curiosity."

"I know you're up to something, Bello. You know can tell me; I can keep a secret." I blushed, imagining the way his mouth looked when he spoke the word curiosity had me...curious.

"I know I can. Are you here yet?"

"Parking right now." I pulled into the nearest spot in front of the small airport and tapped the key fob on my new car that he'd purchased and had delivered to the job a few days ago. According to him, it was a company car, but I didn't know why I needed a company vehicle as a secretary to begin with. At the same time, I wasn't turning down a fully equipped 2020 Mercedes Benz E-Class either.

After being escorted to the tarmac and onto the plane, Vasilios stood until I sat, then took his seat. He smiled warmly as he handed me a flute of champagne, and I promptly sipped the bubbly drink. "Where would you rather be right now: at work being harassed by Cyndi or here with me?"

"Why do you say stuff like that?" I giggled, considering that not only had he lured me out of work, but he was also the person who paid me. Did that make it wrong?

"I speak facts, Kharynn. You know I'm right."

"I guess." I sighed, shifting my gaze to look out the window.

"You guess, huh. What are you thinking, love? Tell me." His words comforted me right when I needed it.

If I was being honest with myself, I was still a little flustered from Charles's phone call earlier. I didn't like how he handled me, and I was trying hard not to take my irritation out on Vasilios. "Nothing important."

"Nothing important, huh." He scratched his beard; those observant pauses of his would often travel past my physical body clear through to my soul. Vasilios had a way of laying eyes on me that made me feel that he knew exactly what I was thinking, and sometimes I was a little scared. My thoughts and emotions were laid out in the open for him to see and inspect, determining whether or not I was worthy of his time. "I see."

"Do you?"

"Pardon me?"

"You say you see, but do you really 'see'? Or are you assuming?" I switched my focus back to the clouds as they floated lazily below my feet, chuckling bitterly to myself.

Again, I felt he was giving me another one of his mesmerizing glances with the expression of a man weighing his options before he spoke. "Kharynn, look at me."

"Vasilios—" I'd overstepped my boundaries, and I knew it. "I'm sorry—"

"Look at me Kharynn." Following his command, I shifted my gaze to where he sat stoically. "Why would you ask a question like that?"

"Nothing." I shook uncontrollably; unable to stop the tears pooling in the corners of my orbs if I wanted to. "Nothing but everything."

"I'm a good listener." If there was one thing I knew for certain about him, Vasilios genuinely cared with no expectations. I wasn't used to that. What I was used to was when I expressed that I was going through something emotionally, the person who should have comforted me didn't. I didn't seek out that type of man, but it would have been nice if they had. A simple 'it's gonna be ok' before changing the subject wasn't cutting it for me anymore.

"I was dating this guy, Charles," I began.

"Ok. Charles. Your ex."

"We had been together for a while, so we had a pretty good idea of each other's faults. So, one day we were at my house. We'd just finished making love and he pinched one of my little fat rolls around my hips," I purposely shifted my arm in from of my stomach so he wasn't staring at the spare tire hanging from my waist as I told my story. "Jokingly, I asked him if I should get a tummy tuck because it bothered me. Not often, but sometimes it does."

"What did he say?"

"He told me he'd find out where his wife went after she gave birth to their twins and pay half," I whispered, dropping my head in embarrassment. "This man had just seen me naked, what was he thinking about me when he was on top of me? I knew then that I wasn't that special; I thought I meant something more to him, you know? Like there was something about me that he couldn't live without. That was a punch to my spirit that I can now say that I never really got over."

Vasilios moved closer to where I sat, tears quietly streaming down my cheeks. "Kharynn, I can't speak for this Charles person. What I can say with certainty is that a woman deserves to be loved without having to give her body to a man first. And if he has a problem with her body, he should allow her the opportunity to be with someone who will love her as she is. I see you and I see a woman who is the embodiment of beauty just as she is, flaws and all."

"Even with this gut?"

"You know, if a woman ever feels she has to change something about herself while she's with me then I have failed as a man and a life partner for not making her feel more than enough."

Vasilios's words rocked me to my core; I had no comeback for that. After that conversation with Charles, I went and bought waist trainers, flat tummy tea…anything that would give me a flatter side profile without having major surgery. I became even more self-conscious in my skin because of him. He'd pretend like it didn't bother him, but when he kept leaving the seven-day complimentary passes to L.A. Fitness on my dresser, I knew it did.

With Vasilios, it was all so complicated, yet so simple. There were no 'buts', no 'what ifs'. No rebuttal. For the duration of our flight, I felt the need to unload all my problems on him for his inspection. I told him about my parents, shared with him my past relationships, I wanted to be free of my past. I wanted him to know everything about me so that there were no secrets between us and go from there. Judging by the look on his face, I already planned on packing up my desk and crawling back to Southwest with my tail tucked between my legs. "I shouldn't—shouldn't have told you that about me."

To my surprise, he pulled me closer, wrapping his arms around my waist. "Kharynn, let me explain something to you, love." We walked together off the plane and instantly I was smacked in the face by the smell of the salty sea air. "Now I'm no expert, but I've been around women for the majority of my adult life. I said that to say there is no cookie-cutter answer when it comes to being in an adult relationship with another adult."

"So, what's the secret?" I probed.

"No secret. You just gotta take the initiative to get to know the other person and make them feel appreciated at all times. Above all, don't play games, let them know your intentions. Now like I said before, I can't speak for this Charles person. What I can say is that in relationships, interest is continuously reciprocated so that the other person doesn't have to constantly validate themselves with an endless pursuit of someone they have no interest in."

I pondered his words, mentally applying them to my own life. Once when I was younger, I overheard my mother on the phone with someone, who I guess was venting about their own failed relationship. I'll never forget the advice my mother gave: *any relationship you're in with somebody that you can't talk to about your feelings, standards, or expectations wasn't solid to begin with.* For once in my life, I just wanted to love someone with all of me and not look stupid.

"Uhmm, Vasilios? Where are we?"

"Charleston. I know a place near the ocean where they have the best shrimp and grits in the low country," he quickly switched back to his carefree self. "And I might have something planned for later on."

"Something like what?" I ruffled my curly locks playfully, putting a twist in my hips like I always did when I walked slightly ahead of him.

"Ahhh…now if I told you that it wouldn't be a secret, now would it?" he growled sexily behind me as he enjoyed the show.

Vasilios

Everybody has a past; how they allow it to affect their present is what determines their future. Kharynn had a lot of baggage, starting with the relationship her parents had with her and with one another and ended with this Charles person. By the time she finished telling me her story, this beauty was in tears. Little did she know if I told her mine, we'd still be on my private jet.

 I took her face in my hands after she let it all out. She'd laid herself out for me to see, trusting that I wouldn't be another person who'd come in her life to set her up for yet another disappointment. Knowing the wall she'd placed around her heart, I knew right then I had to show her something she'd been missing. Years of scouring this earth looking for the right one to carry my legacy and I found someone I wasn't looking for. I fell for a woman I didn't have to take care of, at least not physically. From this point on, I was going to do everything in my power to take care of her.

After we had brunch at this little eatery I liked, I took her shopping to grab something so she could be more comfortable tonight. "Are you enjoying yourself?" I questioned as we walked hand in hand out of the mall.

"Yes, I am," she yawned, rotating her neck as we strolled along. "Just a little tired I guess, what with being whisked away to another state for brunch and all."

"As a former flight attendant, I would think that you would be used to being whisked away on a whim." I stopped on the sidewalk and tilted her head upwards to stare in her eyes. Kharynn's relaxed expression was begging for me to take her back to my house nestled on the banks of the water's edge and show her how a woman of her stature should be treated now, forever and always. "Sleepy?"

"I think I just need a nap." With slightly drooping eyelids, she took a deep breath in and blew it out. "Can we go to the hotel now?" she gathered her lips into the sexiest pout.

"Hotel…sure."

A low and pleasant hum warmed my blood as we reached the grey Mercedes Benz Connect and the driver opened the door. I helped her in first, then passed her bags to the driver to take care of as I took the seat next to hers. She wasn't lying when she said she was tired, Kharynn was already tucked comfortably against the window breathing deeply. I pushed a strand of hair away from her face, admiring her beauty as she slept. I could stare at Kharynn for days and never get bored.

Listening to her slight snores, I ran my fingers through her hair, ogling her chest as it rose and fell. If I could convince her to stay the weekend, it would be easier for me to show her how a man should treat a woman when he said he loved her. She deserved that above all.

I heard a ring tone go off and automatically reached for my phone only to find out it was hers. Kharynn stirred slightly in her sleep but didn't budge. From the vibration associated with each ring, somehow her phone managed to slip halfway out of her purse before it stopped and started again. Out of pure curiosity, I peeked over her shoulder at the screen, thinking it might be urgent. I wasn't surprised to see this Charles person who she just told me about earlier.

Knowing my power and reach, I briefly debated visiting this guy, similar to the one I paid the housewife in Georgia. I was feeling antsy, and there were two ways for me to get the release my inner self craved. Only this time instead of frightening a victim to death, I was gonna love on the one whose chest heaved invitingly to my senses.

"Kharynn wake up." I gave her a gentle nudge when we pulled into my circular driveway. "We're here."

"Where…" she frowned a little before adjusting her eyes to the light. "Vasilios, where are we?"

"This is my private home. On occasion, I come here to think, something about the waves crashing against the shore under the moonlight puts everything into perspective."

"I'll bet." She took everything in with her eyes and I smirked at her relaxed words. This woman knew what she was doing to me with every step. "What else do you do here?"

"What do you mean?" I tapped the code in on the door's keypad and watched her thick frame pass through the threshold.

"As big and beautiful as this home is…Vasilios you expect me to believe you aren't married, aren't in a relationship…you're not even dating?" she rolled her shoulders to ease the tension from sleeping in one spot during our drive. "I don't believe it."

"This little cottage?" Her amazement elicited a lopsided grin from me as our footsteps echoed throughout the living room against the gold veined marble flooring. "It's nothing spectacular."

"Nothing spectacular?" she quizzed. "You have…you know what. Never mind."

"Let me show you to your bedroom." I ushered her upstairs to the bedroom next to mine. My senses told me to take her to my room and show her how I've felt about her since that day on the plane, but my mind said I needed to take it slow. In this case, I decided to go with my mind.

"Vasilios, this is beautiful." I sensed her breath once it caught in her throat, eyes widening while she drunk in the view. Plush white carpet lined the floor as a stark contrast to the room's dark walls with gold trim. The designer draped a furry white throw blanket over the dark grey silk brocaded chaise lounge chair near the window, complimenting the white silk sheets covered by a dark grey bedspread. Tall glass statuesque lamps covered with dark gold satin shades broke up the masculine feel to the room. For this space, I insisted the designer suspend a crystal chandelier from the ceiling, which was textured in a soft white Venetian plaster. The afternoon sun streamed through the floor to ceiling French doors that opened out onto a balcony overlooking the jut of dunes framing the view of the ocean. "I'm moving in."

"You can." If she thought I was gonna tell her no, she thought wrong. I wanted her to move in this house, the condo in Atlanta, my home in Fuquay, my sprawling mansion in Mandeville, my estate in Lagos...

"Why me?"

"Why not you?" I pulled her closer to me and ran my fingertip down her cheek.

"After everything I told you about me...I don't understand."

"Kharynn, why do you think you felt compelled to tell me your life story on the plane? Why do you think I moved my executive team around to accommodate your request for a temporary position? Why do you think I made a phone call to the vice president of human resources at Southwest?"

"To be nice?"

"You've seen me with my staff, do you think I'm that nice?"

"I thought that was your work persona," she ran a confused hand across the back of her neck. "Vasilios—"

"There's something you need to know about me," I began before her ringing phone spoiled the mood.

She fished deep in her bag retrieved her device, glancing at the screen before she slid the button to the right. "I put you on do not disturb, how are you calling me Charles?" She put a finger up for me to hold that thought as she stepped into an adjoining bathroom.

"Access to your cloud, love," he sneered in her ear, unaware my hearing was a lot keener than most. "What the hell are you doing in Charleston?"

"I could've sworn you said we were through, Charles!" she hissed through gritted teeth. "Why the hell are you snooping around my iCloud?"

"Kharynn, I'm sorry."

"What?"

"I said I'm sorry. I was wrong."

"What are you apologizing for, Charles?"

"The way I've treated you. I'm sorry for yelling, sorry for the accusations…I'm sorry for everything. It's hard when you have so many people looking up to you…you don't understand."

"I don't understand what?"

"Between you, the job, my personal life…" he gave her that fake sigh that men gave when they wanted sympathy, "…it's a lot,

Kharynn. It's not just you, I've taken my frustrations out on Eden and the kids too. I shouldn't have yelled at you earlier, and I shouldn't have treated you like I did the last time we saw each other. I know you might never forgive me…"

Damn, he just hit her with the okey-doke, I mused to myself, wondering what her response would be.

"I accept your apology," she whispered lowly. "Charles I—"

"If nothing else, we have a history, babe," he continued. "I know you might be upset with how I handled you, and I don't blame you. But we had some good times though, right? Remember when we went to Costa Rica and it poured down rain on our beach brunch?"

"I remember that," she giggled softly. "You over there smiling and still trying to feed me them wet eggs."

"Can we talk when you get back?" he chuckled in her ear.

She hesitated for a second…in that second, I hoped her response would be… "I'm open to hearing what you have to say."

Not exactly what I was expecting, considering this man wasn't even in my league, but he was right about one thing: they had a history. I let them finish up their conversation because by the time she got back, she wouldn't remember him nor anyone else from her old life. I had to thank Charles when we got back to Atlanta, because of his inability to let go of what's mine, we were making this official tonight.

Chapter 8

Kharynn

When I pulled into the parking lot at Peachtree-Dekalb executive airport a few hours ago, I knew exactly what I wanted. Charles and I were done, and I was open to explore the possibilities with Vasilios. I'd told him things about myself that I'd never shared with anyone, not to mention I felt safe in his space. My life was easier with Bello in it; I didn't have to put on the fake persona that I saved for everyone else when we were together. I could be me.

However, the phone call I'd just finished with Charles had me rethinking my haste to get out of Atlanta and spend time with Vasilios at his four-bedroom 'cottage' with a fountain in the front and swimming pool in the back built on a few acres of oceanfront. My mind told me to forget about Charles and his half-assed apology, but my heart wanted to see what else he had to say.

I hugged my phone closer to my chest confused as ever, not wanting to make a rash decision in the battle waged by my heart that my head would later regret. I had to find Vasilios and let him know I needed to get back to Atlanta. There was something about the tone in Charles's voice…for the first time since we've been together, he sounded truly apologetic. I'd been waiting on that from him for so long…and now I wanted to explore that. Spending this time with Vasilios let me know that I'd shortchanged myself, I deserved to give love and receive love from others. "Vasilios?"

"In here love," his voice came from somewhere behind me. "What's wrong?"

I followed his tenor and ended up at the entrance to the room next to mine. "I don't want to—" I stopped to enjoy the view. If I wasn't in love with this house when I stepped through the doors in my room, I was when I walked through the set of double doors leading me to his. His king-sized bed was situated on a dark grey accent wall adjacent to floor to ceiling windows. On either side of the bed sat two dark wood nightstands which also matched the polished wood table flanked by high backed chairs near the fireplace. Vibrant colored paintings covered one surface of the room where a small mini-bar with liquors I'd never heard of was recessed into a cabinet built smack in the middle of the wall. My eyes were drawn to the muted light from the tray ceiling that bathed the room in a soft glow. "…interrupt."

"You're not interrupting," he called out again, appearing from nowhere with a towel wrapped around his waist. "Just got out the shower, had to smell good for you on our date tonight."

"Oh yea." I fidgeted with my hands, not sure whether to tell him I had to go or run my hand down his hard, rippling abs. "Our date."

"Family emergency?"

"Uhmm…" It didn't feel right lying to him, and I hadn't told it yet. "That was my ex on the phone."

"Oh?"

"Yeah. He wants to talk when I get back."

"Hmmm."

"I was wondering—"

"You want to go home?" he asked before disappearing into what I assumed was his closet.

"Vasilios, I know it's crazy but—"

"No problem. I understand." He gave me a tight smile as he picked up his phone and sent a text. "I'll call the driver to take us back to the airport."

I felt a pang stab at my heart; after everything he said this afternoon it was that simple to get rid of me? "That easy, huh."

"Kharynn, I'm not into playing games. I brought you here because I wanted to build something with you, show you how valuable you are." He pulled a shirt over his head as he spoke. "Give you something that no woman can ever say she's received. If you're looking for someone who's gonna crowd you, be all in your space begging for your time just to walk all over you again to appease their ego, that's not me." His text ringer dinged a second time and he walked over to where I stood good and verbally slapped. "Ready?"

"How crazy would you think I was if I told you I wanted to stay?"

"Don't forget to grab your purse. I'll meet you downstairs." He slid past me and jogged sideways down the circular staircase.

I slouched down the steps after I grabbed my bag from 'my bedroom', thinking about his words. Charles had thrown a monkey wrench in my weekend; I was supposed to be getting ready for my date with Bello. A part of me told me he'd done so on purpose, especially since he had no idea of who I'd gone to Charleston with. If he truly had access to the cloud on my phone, I wondered why he hadn't called Vasilios.

I wanted a do-over. Judging from Bello's mood as he held my door open, I needed to talk fast. "I guess that's a no, huh?" I chuckled nervously.

"Guess so." He slammed the door behind me. I heard his footfalls walk around the vehicle to the other side; my heart dropped when he plopped down in the front seat. "Buckle up."

"Vasilios."

"Yeah."

"Can you please sit back here with me so we can talk?"

"At this age, I'm only interested in consistency, stability, respect, and loyalty. You and your ex seem to enjoy playing this game of gaslighting to guilt-trip the other one back into the relationship and I don't have the patience for pettiness. Once feelings get involved, there's nothing that can change that unless the person wants to change."

"I made a bad judgment call for a second. Are you gonna hold that against me?"

My eyes skimmed his profile from the back seat. His shoulders seemed to fall in defeat as he took a deep breath in and let it out. "Kharynn, you deserve someone who isn't embarrassed to love you. You deserve someone who tells their friends about how wonderful and beautiful you are. You deserve someone who wants to take selfies with you to look at when they miss you. You deserve someone who loses sleep to be there for you, to tell you how much they love you. I need you to understand that I'm here. I would never hurt you like he did." Vasilios spoke quietly.

His words hit home for me; Charles wouldn't utter anything even remotely close to Vasilios's musings. Why was I allowing this man so much power over my life, to pick me up when he wanted to play with me and put me down when he didn't? The familiar complacency that came with Charles had me out here looking like a fool; I could only imagine what my co-workers whose hearts he also played with on a whim said about me behind my back. "I know."

"No, you don't. And until you realize it fully, I don't think we should spend time in each other's space."

"Are you firing me, Vasilios?"

"No, stay as long as you want. I rarely work out of the Atlanta office anyway; the majority of my work is done right here," he waved his phone in the air. "If you do decide to leave, can you give me at least two weeks' notice? I need time to find your replacement."

Oh, he's serious. "I can do that."

"Thanks."

We were both quiet for the remainder of the ride and boarding the plane back to Atlanta. Stealing glances in his direction as he purposely avoided my gaze, I wished I knew what he was thinking. What did he mean when he said he wanted to give me something that no woman can ever say she received?

I want to give you me, Kharynn, I heard in my thoughts. Glancing again in his direction, I saw his brooding expression hadn't changed, yet I heard his voice loud and clear. *No woman in this lifetime can say she's had my heart like you do,* I listened while watching him, not seeing his lips separate. "Vasilios, I know you aren't speaking to me, but I think there was something in that drink at brunch—"

"It wasn't." His lips moved this time. "I told you that I had something to tell you before your ex called."

"What?"

"Kharynn, there's a lot you don't know about me."

"Like the fact that you're a ventriloquist?" I giggled, but he didn't even crack a smile. "Vasilios?"

Now it was his turn to take a deep breath in and blow it out, slowly choosing his words. "Remember when we first met? Not on the plane, but our first official meeting?"

"Yea, at the Waffle House."

"No, in your bathroom." He leaned forward to look directly into my eyes. "When you were in the bubble bath that evening after our flight."

"What…what are you saying?"

The curiosity in his eyes had me hypnotized, touching back on my thoughts that night. "Do you remember?"

"I—I do, but…"

"I'm going to cut to the chase. Kharynn, I'm what your kind refers to as a vampire."

"A what?" I sat back in my seat, giggling for a second before I busted out laughing. "Next you're gonna tell me Vasilios is your middle name and Dracula is your first! Stop playing, Bello."

"I knew you'd say that," he turned his gaze back to the beginning of the sunset slightly obscured by billowy clouds. *Just as I said then, I'll say it again, you not ready for me.*

"I am ready—wait, how do you do that?" I insisted. Vasilios wasn't a damn vampire. Vampires only existed in Hollywood and Bram Stoker's novels.

Unless you're unknowingly trapped in a Bram Stoker novel, I can assure you I am very real, his voice traveled through the synapses in my brain. *Would you like to see my fangs too?*

"Yeah, show me your fangs," I chided, only to see how far he'd take this little game of his.

You don't have to speak aloud, I know what you're thinking, he whispered to my mind's eye. *In time, Kharynn. In time.*

Everything's in time; you tell me you're a vampire but can't prove it to me now. Tell me I'm not ready for you— my face frowned thinking of all the things I wanted to yell at him.

You're on your way back to see your ex after I took you to Charleston fully prepared to fuck the shit outta you until the sun rose behind the dunes, yet I'm the one who has something to prove, he expressed. *All this time you been eye raping me, now all of a sudden you miss ya ex.*

As much time as we'd spent together, he'd never once brought up sex. I mean yea, we kissed a few times, but nothing more than that. We usually went somewhere and vibed, enjoying each other's company. I had an idea, but I didn't know THAT was how he felt about me. "Can we go back?" I thought I wanted to hear Charles out, but if it came down to talking to him or seeing Vasilios naked…

He glanced at me sideways, snickering smugly while shifting his manhood. *Nah. Go back to Atlanta and hear Charles out.*

You want me to go back without giving me a chance to explain myself? I questioned mentally, sliding closer to where he sat. Reaching over to stroke his wood, I nibbled softly against his earlobe.

What you got to say? he asked nonchalantly, leaning his head back against the headrest.

I just want to apologize for being so flaky, I ran my hands up and down the outside of his pants where his sinewy member began to rise to attention. *You know I think about you sometimes.*

When do you think about me, Kharynn? he breathed. I felt his hand wrap around the back of my neck while he simultaneously bit his lip.

When I'm alone, in my bed. I think about you a lot, I shared, quickening my stroke.

Tell me what goes through your mind, his lustful thoughts shone in his eyes as I decided to slip my hand inside his slacks. Quickly undoing his belt buckle, Vasilios helped by unbuttoning and unzipping his pants, so I had more room to work. Allowing my fingertips to graze his tip, I stuck my tongue in his ear, continuing our game.

"Mmm…how you would feel inside of me," I whispered in his ear, twirling my tongue across his lobe. "Wondering how you would taste when you exploded in my mouth…filling me up with thick, sweet—" I breathed as he leaked precum onto my fingertips. I outlined his jawline using my mouth before my lips met his, my hands tracing the tip of his man pole with his juices. My womanly fluids flowed freely as I peck-kissed my way around his lips; I ran my fingernails gently across the back of his neck while preparing for him to consummate our growing attraction.

His hand was warm sliding up the back of my leg, circling my kneecap, up and around my thighs his fingertips danced, slipping underneath my dress on his way to my erogenous zone.

"Who told you to wear panties today," he growled while I trembled with anticipation. Temptation overtook my senses; I was ready for whatever. I cupped his twin sacks in my left hand while making a soft fist with my right so I could tug on his stiff member. My eyes fluttered closed once his two slipped swiftly between my rose petals. "Kharynn, don't start nothing you can't finish."

"I rarely do." I quickly straddled him in one move as he ripped my panties free. Positioning myself above his long, thick pole, Vasilios briefly rubbed the tip of his man candy across my vulva before ramming himself forcefully into my wet slit. "Mmphf," I quickly adjusted to his girth. If this what it was like making love to a 'vampire', I'd deprived myself far too long.

"Ooouuu…" he gripped my shoulders tightly as his belt buckle dug into my butt cheeks. "Come get this vampire dick…mmmm…"

"Bello!" I whimpered his name during our moment of rhapsody, committing each stroke of his shaft inside my womb to memory. Unable to contain myself, I sunk my teeth into his shoulder blade, feeling him delve deeper and deeper between my dewy folds was nothing short of divine intoxication.

"Mine, Kharynn," he grunted in my ear, his sweat splattered across my body with each thrust. "Do you hear me? MINE, Kharynn!"

"YOURS, Vasilios," I wheezed, bouncing precariously on his man pole as he slammed inside of me with vigor. "All yours baby."

"You promise?" his voice changed; his tenor deeper as his chest broadened against my breasts.

I promise, I spoke silently through my thoughts. His arms gripped me tighter…so tight I could barely breathe.

Stay with me, Kharynn. Stay with me forever…

*I will…*I managed to form the thought before I felt his fangs pierce my neck…

Vasilios

Kharynn was an exquisite lover, the care she showed me…how she put me first…truthfully, I wasn't expecting that from her. In the heat of passion, I brought her into my realm…to life as an immortal being. Once I sunk my fangs into the protruding vein in her neck, she was mine…all mine and there was nothing she could do about it. Her cry filled with pain and agony only made me want her more, her warm elixir melted any doubt I might've had about meshing her existence to mine. Kharynn changed my mind on how I should love a woman, and now she belonged to me forever.

She was still knocked out when we got back to Atlanta, so I carried her off the plane to my personal vehicle. I knew she would be out of it once she came to, and I had a lot to explain. Life as she used to know it had now changed for her; the way she moved, her senses, diet…everything. Granted, she wasn't a bloodthirsty creature of the night preying unsuspecting victims, but she would move to a vegan diet, for us any flesh was a delicacy. As my partner in eternity, she had access to some of the more affluent lifeblood the world had to offer, so she had no need to pursue and kill a living being unless it was for sport.

"Vasilios…" Kharynn's voice called faintly to me from my bedroom. Gathering her sustenance of a warm kale salad and a glass of apple juice, I went to feed my lady love.

"I brought you something for your headache." I soothed, placing the tray of food in front of her. While Kharynn raked the fork across her salad, thoughts of my own salvation came to mind:

Death hung thickly in the air around me as my eyes darted back and forth from the man standing in front of me to the throng of people behind him. Forced to stand and watch in horror as my mother's skin melted from her bones, I cringed inwardly seeing her hand reach out in agony for someone...anyone to save her from the hell of being burned at the stake. As the elders from the village nodded their heads in agreement for their heinous actions, one of the women pointed to me.

"Aye, the child! The child is of she!" she screamed; her pale, bony finger served as an accusatory death sentence. "Burn the child! Burn the child!" she chanted.

The one person who I knew would not allow that to happen was now a pile of ashes blowing in the winds across the tall grass of Stephens Field. Fear cemented my feet to the ground; the scream stuck in my throat slowly transformed into a thick lump of terror as they moved closer to where I stood. "Burn the child! Burn the child!" the villagers joined her in her role of judge, jury, and executioner. I was an unwilling victim of my mother's crimes for which I needed to atone.

Out of nowhere, the wind picked up as a whooshing sound flew overhead, panic-stricken cries of hysteria washed over the villagers at the sky full of stars now turned pitch black. I was swept off my feet as a frantic scream pierced the air; a lone makeshift torch was thrown haphazardly in my direction as I sailed off above the treetops. While on my late-night voyage across the tall grass and dark waters, I felt a pang of hunger while I was simultaneously pricked on the side of my neck.

Alighting on a nearby tree, the mysterious figure lowered me gingerly onto a nearby branch before taking off into serendipitous moonlight. I was left alone in the treetops until the sun's rays traversed across the eastern side of the land with the coming of the new day. I heard movement behind me too late; a second prick in the same spot soothed the dizzying hunger pains in my belly. The leaves from the mighty oak tree where I'd found myself stranded whispered that I was now immortal, and no harm would befall me on this day nor any other before I was left to my own devices...

"How are you feeling?" I blinked my way back to the present where she sat up in the bed watching me like a hawk.

"Oh...my head is killing me," she shared, her eyes never wavering as she took a small bite of her food. "What...what happened?"

"What's the last thing you remember?"

"The last thing I remember," she took a deep breath in and blew it out. "I remember us making love at 30,000 feet. The way my thighs are aching, please tell me that happened," she giggled, blushing.

"Yes love, that happened." I leaned over to kiss her rosy cheek. "Anything after that?"

"No," she shook her head, still confused. "All I know is that everything on me hurts. And I'm starving for some strange reason."

"Finish your food first, then we'll talk, ok?" I encouraged. "There's a lot that you need to know."

"Vasilios?"

"Yes?"

"Am I a vampire?" she rubbed the two small lumps on her neck, waiting for my response.

"Not fully, but—"

"Why? Why would you do that to me!" she exploded.

"What?"

"I don't want to be a vampire!"

"You…what?" I was confused. "I did what you asked!"

"I ASKED you to be a vampire, Vasilios?"

"No, but…"

"What makes you think everyone wants your life! Flying around, sucking on dirty necks, God only knows how many diseases you have! Wait…do you have…" she rambled hysterically.

"STOP!" I roared; I wasn't in the mood for her accusations. "Kharynn, maybe you need a little more time…" I stood up, tenting my fingers in front of my face while staring at the shocked expression on hers.

"Change me back, Vasilios! NOW!"

"You think it's that easy? You think I just snap my fingers and you're mortal? No baby, it doesn't work like that!"

"Well, since you said I'm not fully a vampire, don't do whatever it is that you do to make me one! I can live with being half-mortal and half a regular human being," she picked up her fork to finish her meal, still fuming.

"Doesn't work like that either, Kharynn. See, books and Hollywood have you thinking that you'll just hang in the balance until the end of your days. Live a nice, regular, boring, vanilla life until it's your time. You feel that tightness in your forehead? Appetite changed? Lemme get you a nice, juicy, medium-rare steak instead of that salad…"

"I think I'm going to throw up," she jumped up and bolted to the bathroom. After giving her stomach the relief it deserved, she washed her mouth and crept back in the room quietly. "What did you do to me?"

"Kharynn, I did what you asked. I said you were mine, you agreed. I asked if I could have you forever and you said yes. Where I'm from, they call that consent."

"What's happening to me, Vasilios?"

"You're dying. If I don't give you the anti-serum, you'll be dead in twenty-four hours." I spoke truthfully.

"And if you do?"

"How old do I look to you, Kharynn?"

Her hand trembled dragging across my face; her mouth scrunched up in a scowl. "Uhmm…if I had to guess, somewhere between 32 and 38."

"I'll be three hundred and forty-four years old on my birthday this year."

"What?"

"Am I too old for you?"

"No, it's not that…" she arched an eyebrow in disbelief. "Three hundred and forty-four though?"

"Well, you know what they say: black don't crack," I chuckled, trying to lighten the mood.

She ran both hands down my smooth face in amazement. "It sure doesn't."

"I told you that to say that you'll still have human traits. I don't know much about this whole thing, but I can tell you that although I age a lot slower than mortals, I do age."

"What else can you do?"

"Well, you've seen me during the daytime, so that whole sleeping in a coffin thing is bullshit," I counted on my fingers. "I've been shot with silver bullets, stabbed by so many blessed crosses I've lost count, burned at a few stakes, drowned, buried alive...pretty much everything except blown up or chopped into pieces which I try to avoid. I've gone to church, showered in holy water, and I enjoy garlic butter on my lobster."

"Vasilios...I'm...I don't know what to say."

"Say you'll stay with me, Kharynn." I scrutinized her face to get a beat on her emotions, taking note of her panic-stricken expression. If she decided on the latter, I didn't think I could live with myself.

"Where...where is this anti-serum stuff?"

"Kharynn...I don't want you to do this if you don't want to. Had I gotten any inkling that you were against it, any notion that you weren't genuine when you said you wanted to be with me forever, I wouldn't have gone through with it." I spoke honestly.

"But if I don't, I'll—"

"Yes."

"Then I guess I have no other choice then," she looked away bitterly. "Everything I've ever lived for is gone, my hopes, my dreams…"

"Let me give you hope. We can make new dreams together, then spend our days making them come true, my love," I sat on the bed with her face cupped between my palms. "Kharynn, you complete me. Let me complete you."

"Vasilios…" she couldn't stop the wetness leaking slowly from her orbs. "I'm scared. I'm so scared, what if you don't—"

"I'll always love you, Kharynn. Neither you nor anyone else can ever change that," I tried to put her mind at ease. She laid her head on my shoulder; the two small pricks where I'd initially declared my love for her shone in the muted light. Dragging my tongue across the pink scars, I pulled her body closer to mine as she wept softly to herself. "Baby—"

"Do it, Vasilios."

"Are you—"

"VASILIOS! DO IT!"

Following her demand, I inhaled her scent of curiosity and fear. Excitement coursed deep in my loins; my fangs dropped a second time before I sank my canine teeth in her trembling flesh.

Chapter 9

Kharynn

I awoke to darkness in Vasilios's bed; my throat dry but I wasn't thirsty. Rubbing my hand across the silken sheets, I discovered I was alone. Ever since I got bit, my senses had been heightened in triplicate; but the one thing my body craved was his scent. I could feel the blood coursing through each vein, the thoughts jumbled in my head that I used to ignore were now a manageable hum. My ears picked up on the cars swooshing past on the interstate, and I couldn't help but to wonder how close or far away we were.

Instead of calling his name, innately I knew to whiff the air and it would lead me to him. I stepped onto the stepstool placed next to the California King sized bed that sat high off the floor in the direction where he was. Moving down another step, my eyes adjusted quickly to the darkness as I traveled through the halfway closed door. I stepped into the bathroom to his masculine scent mixed with sandalwood, vanilla, and soy. The tub full of bubbles surrounded by scented candles beckoned me closer and I acquiesced to the water's request. Deciding to not wait for permission, I removed his t-shirt sticking to my skin and stepped down into the water, my eyes closed as his smell came closer to where I sat.

"Who told you it was okay for you to get in my bathwater?" his deep voice gently kissed my earlobes.

"I did. Who told you it was okay for you to get out of my bed?"

"My apologies, queen," I heard him disrobe before he slid behind my back to join me in the mountainous bubble terrain. "I thought you might need somebody to wash this body of yours." His hands moved lightly across my breasts as he spoke.

"Mmm…next time ask for permission first," I opened my eyes when he nuzzled his lips against my shoulder.

"With your permission," he sang in my ear, "I wanna spend the night sipping on you. Gimme that green light Kharynn," he groaned, slipping two wet fingers inside my soft flesh.

"Go, Vasilios…mmm…go, go, go…" I moaned as he stroked my most secret place.

"It's all about you tonight love," he grunted, his warm breath ragged in my ear. "Do you like it when I kiss you?"

"Mmhmm…" I moaned, winding my hips back and forth against his masculine fingers. "Will you kiss me? Please?"

Vasilios grabbed my chin and tilted my head to one side before he placed his tongue against my skin. His expert touch assaulted my senses; hungrily he took possession of my mouth. Once his lips brushed across mine for the third time, my tongue instantly made damp trails across his. My bottom lip swelled with passion; I had to stop…this relationship had to be about more than the insatiable lust that drew me to him like iron to a magnet.

We exchanged seductive glances as I pulled myself up to sit on the edge of the tub; I needed to get away from him to collect my bearings, even if it was just for a second. "Vasilios what are we doing?"

"I'm making love to you, my sweet…" his sinfully smooth lips circled my kneecap, "…sweet…" his tongue trailed up the inside of my thigh, "…soon to be bride…" Raising himself, he kneeled in front of me to press his lips against mine for a second time. "Are you gonna deny me you?"

"No…I…"

His fingers stroked gentle butterfly wings across my slippery inner thighs before he replaced his touch with his flesh. I felt his breath expel faintly against my lips in a slow, steady stream as mine quickened in my throat. No words were exchanged as his bulbous tip strained against my bare vulva, trembling as she allowed him entry. Submerged between my thighs, his thick shaft blossomed into a rock-hard masterpiece; my chocolate Michelangelo sculpted sensuous works of art between my thighs. "Kharynn…"

"Vasilios, what are you doing to me, love…" I pitched and retracted against his hips as he returned the favor. "Mmm…"

"Work that pussy…mmm, I wish you could feel how tight she gripping me," he grunted lowly. "She gets wet while you sleep too, did you know that?"

"No," escaped my lips; my eyes rolled to the back of my head when his palm smoothed across my stomach, up through the valley between my breasts, and stopping at the base of my neck.

"You don't want me doing this to you?" he circled his hands underneath my backside to lift me, balancing himself against the slippery water. With my legs wide open, he slid my honey pot back and forth against his dipstick, laser-focused on our skin slamming together and releasing in the candle's wavering light.

"VASILIOS! OOOOOHHH!" I threw my head back, his strong arms held me still. We couldn't keep…oh…

"I love feeling you, Kharynn," he wheezed. "I love being inside of you, sharing your body with mine. This…" I felt his sinewy meat swell up thicker as he pounded me into oblivion, "thisssssssssss….got dammit baby," he moaned with the warmth coursing inside my secret place. "This is you and me. This is us."

"So, what—" That stupid ringtone of his cut me off in mid-sentence. "Who is that, Vasilios?"

"Baby, how am I supposed to know if I'm still inside of you?" he smirked, lowering my feet into the rapidly cooling water. "Wanna answer it?"

"Yea, where is it?" I stepped out of the water about to head towards our adjoining bedroom. "Scared I might find out something about you that you didn't want me to know?"

"No, I need to dry you off first. You got bubbles on that perfect ass that I love to watch walk away." He patted the droplets from my skin as I stood in front of the steps to the bathtub fuming. "Now you can go, Mrs. Bello."

"Don't think because you called yourself giving me your last name that this is over with." I took off in the direction of his ringing phone when it stopped. His steps matched mine as he came up behind me when his phone sang for a second time. "Hmph, must be important, huh." I snatched the device from the charging pad on the table. Sliding my finger across the sensored glass, I put the phone to my ear and breathed in the speaker, not saying anything.

"Hello?" Cyndi's voice crooned in my ear. "Bello, we need to talk. Now. Tonight."

"About what?" I demanded to know. He wasn't leaving my bed to go see anybody, much less his old secretary.

"Who is this?" she snapped, her tone matching mine.

Instead of answering her, I handed him the phone. "It's for you, my love."

"Cyndi, why the hell are you calling me at 4 a.m.? I told you a long time ago—"

"Is that how you speak to the mother of your child?" she screamed, making sure I heard her words.

"Cyndi stop with that crazy shit; you know I used a condom!" Vasilios roared in her ear, then paused. The pause…that pregnant pause that sat between a lie and the truth. The truth that was bound to come out regardless of when or how it happened.

"Your child?" My body trembled at her words. At that moment it didn't matter whether they were true, but what it did prove was that he lied to me. "I asked if you and her were in a relationship and you told me no, Bello. You stood in my face, looked me dead in my eyes and told me you never touched her."

I could hear her on the other end of his phone still yapping before he hung up on her in mid-sentence. "Kharynn wait—"

"The only reason," I had to catch my breath because I could feel myself about to lose it, "THE ONLY REASON I went on that date with you is because you promised me, Vasilios. You promised that you and her had never been together!"

"And we weren't!" he pleaded. "We—Kharynn, I swear I…"

"Do you expect me to believe that? VASILIOS YOU JUST SAID—"

"I know what I said! Kharynn wait—can we just…"

"Go to hell, Vasilios!" I pushed him away from me, I couldn't. I couldn't be in his airspace; I couldn't listen to yet another excuse when emotionally I was all in. I couldn't…I couldn't be in another relationship with a substitute for Charles Whitlow.

I stormed across the bedroom searching for my clothes, trying to ignore the pain in my heart that pierced my soul. Vasilios claimed nothing could hurt me, but the stabbing in my chest told me otherwise. Her words were the equivalent to torture swirling in my soul, my heart beat faster in my chest then slowed with the knowledge that this man…THIS MAN was the cause of an agony like no other. Vasilios wasn't the one who was supposed to hurt me. He wasn't supposed to…

"Kharynn, don't shut me out like this. Please," I dodged his advances, refusing to hear his explanation. "Can I explain?"

"What? Huh? What do you have to say, Charles! This woman said she's the mother of your child! How do you expect me to deal with that?"

"Charles, huh." He backed away from where I stood with all the heat, ready to burn him alive and reduce him to ashes. "Yea, maybe we both need some time apart."

"Where are my clothes?"

He sat on the bed watching me as I purposely tore his room apart, running a hand across his tapered haircut. Yes, it was petty, but no, I didn't care. In the past twenty-four hours, he'd brought me to the peak of the purest love, then plummeted me into the annals of hatred for everything he stood for. I wanted to snatch his heart out of his chest and rip him into tiny pieces with my bare hands. "Check the corner."

"You're an asshole, you know that? Vasilios, you're such a fucking asshole!"

"You're right, Kharynn." His voice came low and muffled. "I'm an asshole"

I flipped my shirt inside out, not wanting to be remotely perceived as attractive at this moment. I didn't need him reminding me of how cute I was when I made the smallest gesture or touching me…touching me to elicit a reaction from my body as only he could. Who was I kidding these past few weeks? There was no such thing as love and commitment in a relationship. All men cheat, the only thing we women had to look forward to were those moments of stolen passion where nothing mattered but him. Him. HIM.

"You don't get to do that, Vasilios! You don't get to agree with me! As old as you are, man up and take ownership for your actions!"

"Kharynn, she said that to get under your skin! She ain't pregnant!"

"You keep saying she ain't pregnant, but I noticed you not saying you didn't touch her, Vasilios! Just be honest! We're done here!"

"It was one night," he spoke directly to my mind, his voice steady and controlled. *"Kharynn, I swear she meant nothing to me."*

"If that were the case, you wouldn't have lied! YOU WOULDN'T HAVE LIED, VASILIOS!" I screamed in his face at the top of my lungs. "Stay out of my head and out of my life!" With those words, I snatched the front door open and stormed out.

My car was still at the airport, so I had to call an Uber. The elevator sped to the bottom floor at dizzying speed, and with the way I was feeling it could have smashed into the concrete base on the ground floor and ripped me to smithereens. He took everything good in me, everything that I was in the process of healing from, everything that made me who I was and ripped that band-aid off for the world to see. I couldn't deal; Vasilios was worse…way worse than Charles. Vasilios set me up to love him, set me up to love myself and him. Charles would have never—

The elevator hit the ground floor with a gentle bounce that resonated as a thundering BOOM; he never told me my hearing would change.

"AAAHHH!"

As I stood in the corner of the electronic moving box from hell, the wind from the doors sliding open stabbed at my already tender eardrums; I had to cover my ears with open palms. Part of me wanted to go back upstairs and curl up in a ball underneath his Egyptian silk sheets, but the pain in my heart told me no.

I plugged my ears with my fingers and pressed on. The app said my ride was outside, and I needed to get home immediately. I jogged to the silver-colored Chevy Cruise at the curb and appreciated that the car didn't stink when I opened the door. "Thanks for being out this early in the morning, I appreciate it."

"Oh, no problem Kharynn. Buckle up and get comfortable," her voice was kind. If she kept this up, by the end of this ride she was getting five stars and a tip. "Going home?"

"Yea, long day, you know how Fridays are."

"I hear ya."

For the most part, the ride to Chamblee was quiet, and I was finally able to take a normal breath. I wasn't in the mood for small talk with someone I didn't know, choosing instead to sort out my feelings for Vasilios. It could have all been so simple, yet he chose to make it hard. Why couldn't he be honest with me, knowing what I'd gone through from everyone that I thought would protect my heart?

"Daddy, can I go with you? Please?"

"I'll be right back for you baby, aight? Pack your stuff and I'll come over in about an hour."

"Stop lying to her, Isaac. You know you ain't coming back."

"Chelle, if I told my baby girl I'm coming back, then I'll be back. You be ready for me too, we going for a second round..."

My father was never there for me. He only came around to antagonize my mother when he and his wife were on the outs and to dump cum in her when they weren't:

"Stop that damn crying Kharynn, you knew he wasn't coming! Now get your little ass in there and clean that room!"

My abandonment issues as a child led to my naivety as an adult; any time an older man paid me any attention I equated that to mean he wanted me:

"Kharynn, I wanted to talk to you about your grades. I think you'd do a great job as a tutor, and it'll look good on your transcript. I can give you a recommendation.

"And I can give you something else…"

In college, every professor who'd asked me out for coffee I had sex with. Then there was Charles, who I'd been with the longest. He was like the pied piper and I blindly followed him all over the world to fuck:

"You wanted to see me, Charles?"

"Lock the door. Come sit right here. I'm about to put the plane on auto-pilot, open your legs…"

The buildings outside were beginning to look familiar, so I pulled my phone from my bra since I didn't have any pockets nor panties. I wanted to make sure I tipped her now because when I went in the house, that was all she wrote. Sliding my finger across the sensored glass until the Uber app displayed, I then pulled up the ride in progress. "How do you pronounce your name?"

"Eden. Like the Garden of Eden in the bible," she was friendly enough. Studying her picture…those eyes…that smile…it couldn't be…

Eden? Charles's wife?

"Which entrance?" her voice brought me out of my state of shock. Her husband was a well-known and respected pilot, yet she was out driving Uber on a Friday night/Saturday morning?

"Oh, uhmm…you can drop me off right here. I'll…I'll walk."

"You sure?" And she was concerned about my safety. This poor, gentle, unsuspecting woman was the salt of the earth. Charles and Vasilios were both cut from the same asshole cloth as far as I was concerned.

"Yea, I'll be ok. The lot is narrow, and my neighbors can't park." I had to think of a good enough excuse; if she knew like I did she wouldn't care how I got home. Up until six weeks ago, I was having sex with her husband, the least I could do was double her recommended tip on the app. "Thank you."

"Have a good day, Kharynn. Be safe," she called out, ending the ride.

"You too, sis." I waved at her car pulling away from the curb.

Wow. That could have been me.

Vasilios

She left me. She left me sitting in this condo. She left me sitting in this condo alone. She left me sitting in this condo alone and without her. I had her…I had her here and now she was gone. I should've been truthful with her, but at the same time, I didn't want her to think I gave Cyndi that much thought. She was a secretary and a temporary piece of ass. Nothing more and probably less. Where she got the idea in her head that we were a couple I had no idea.

Not only was I missing Kharynn in the flesh, I was missing her in spirit. She was now a part of me, which meant she'd also know if I was reading her thoughts. I wanted to know what was going on in her head, what she was thinking…about me…about us…

My phone was ringing again, but I had no interest in answering. *It might be her…* She ran out so quick I didn't have a chance to tell her about her sensitive hearing and taste buds. She couldn't eat just anything…

"Kharynn?"

"No, it's not your precious Kharynn." Cyndi's whiny voice irked my senses. "I need to know what time you are available tomorrow."

"For?"

"I forgive you for your little fling with your secretary," she continued as if I'd asked for it. "I'll admit that I might not have been fulfilling my duties, and for that, I apologize."

"What duties are those, might I ask?"

"My duties as your girlfriend, silly," she chuckled sweetly. "All this time I've been racking my mind trying to figure out why you've been so short with me. So, tomorrow I have us scheduled to go look at a few places down the street from the office…"

"You're joking, right?"

"Baby, I'm going to need you more than ever with the baby coming—"

"Cyndi, how long are you going to play this game?"

"Game? Vasilios, what—"

"Didn't I—you know what? You're fired."

"Fired? Why—"

"Come in and clean out your desk Monday morning between 9 and 10 a.m. Any time after that and security won't allow you up to the executive suites. Have a nice life, Cyndi."

"Vasilios don't—" I hurried up and clicked off the line. I had to have a meeting with Trina to see if I could fire her for anything that would stick. She would be the second person I officially terminated Monday morning. First on my list was Kharynn Lewis.

"Cyndi is a no-brainer, I was wondering when you'd recognize her subpar performance," Trina plopped down across from me with a grandé cappuccino from Starbucks and her usual slice of warm banana nut bread. "Kharynn though?"

"Off the record?"

"Of course. We were friends prior to you hiring me, Vasilios."

"Ok." I crossed the conference room and checked the hallway. My HR recap meetings were scheduled for 7 a.m. on Monday mornings, two hours before anyone else was scheduled in case we needed to discuss a termination, executive staff included. "I fucked up."

"And fell in love with her, didn't you?" she flashed a knowing smile. Trina was more than the head of human resources; she was the closest thing to a sister that I had. We met one night at a bar in Midtown and hit it off. I found out she'd just been let go from a company that was moving their corporate offices overseas and brought her in. Our company was one of the best in all businesses across the board because of her attention to detail, knowledge of the law, and flexibility with the staff.

"Damn, am I that obvious?" I snickered, smoothing my hand down my dress shirt.

"Well I don't know whether anyone else can tell, but to me, you've been 'that obvious'," she air quoted, "since Kharynn Lewis stepped off the elevator for the first time."

"She gorgeous, Trina," I sighed, leaning back in my chair. "I fell in love with her on that flight from Raleigh, haven't been able to get her out of my head since then."

"Oh, that's the flight attendant you texted me about?"

"That's her."

"I wonder how I missed that." She removed her glasses to pinch the bridge of her nose. "I don't want you to term Kharynn, Vasilios. Not only is she a stellar performer, but I can also see her moving up to take my job."

"Trina, I'm fucking her. How's that gonna look?"

"Then stop. Not only are you setting yourself up for heartbreak, but if it ends up being the other way around, we could very easily be looking at an EEOC investigation."

"If so, fuck it. She can have all this." I dropped my head in my hands for a second time. "None of it matters if I can't have her."

"You're serious, aren't you?"

"I'm dead ass. She my soul mate."

"Was Cyndi your soul mate too?" she giggled, sliding her frames in place.

"Trina, I told you about that the day after it happened. Cyndi was a temporary lapse in judgment."

"See. Your 'temporary lapses in judgment' is the reason we're discussing terming one of the best secretaries you've ever had."

"The best though?"

"The ABSOLUTE best. I don't say anything when she walks out of here on Friday at 12 and don't come back until Monday morning, do I?"

"That was one time."

"That's been every Friday since she's worked here, Vasilios. Which brings me to my second point: Cyndi also knows that. You don't need a sexual harassment lawsuit either."

"You telling me I can't fire either of these women?"

"Tell you what, Vasilios. Keep it in your pants and I'll call the insurance company. If we offer Cyndi a settlement and remind her of the non-disclosure she signed when she hired in, we should be ok."

"And Kharynn?"

"I'll let you handle that." She pushed her chair back from the table preparing to leave, gathering up her notepad and coffee.

"Sis—"

"Don't 'sis' me now; I wasn't sis when you and my favorite employee consummated y'all relationship," she called out behind her. "Keep that same energy, boss!"

Chapter 10

Kharynn

I had to call off for the week because I was still getting used to this whole 'bride of a vampire' life I'd been sucked into, but by Friday I was feeling somewhat better. Trina texted me every day to make sure I was ok and to see if I needed anything. I appreciated her for that, Southwest would've threatened my job if I took more than two days. I saw a Twitter post somewhere that said take your personal days because these jobs don't give a fuck about you. That statement hit home for me more than once working for a major airline.

Since I was unable to do anything for myself, Postmates and Uber Eats were my best friends. According to the app, Javaris was two minutes away, so I dragged myself from my bedroom to the front door so he didn't leave with my food. That happened to me a few days ago; I was in the bathroom praying to the porcelain god and unable to get to the door in time. Next thing I knew my food was gone and I was stuck with a charge from Georgia Diner. They gave me my money back though.

My stomach growled louder when the knock on the door finally came. "Hey, thanks for the—Charles?"

"Kharynn, how you been?"

I looked at the bag with my chicken soup from Chick-fil-A in his hands, confused. First I run into his wife from a rideshare app, now he works for Postmates? Southwest didn't play when they did their investigations. "You driving—"

"What? Oh nah, that guy just handed me this," he held out his arm with my food. Peeking over his shoulder, I saw the red Honda speeding out the lot. "This all you eating?"

"Yea, I haven't been feeling too good. Come in." I faked a cough, hoping he didn't.

"Damn, you ok?" he stepped over the white dress I peeled off on my way to the shower that morning Vasilios pissed me off. "This place is a mess."

"Well hello to you too." I plopped down in the chair adjacent to the front door. I wasn't trying to lead him on, especially since technically he still wasn't welcome in my home. "What do you want?"

Charles sat across from me on the sofa, giving me those sad little puppy dog eyes. "I uhhh—"

"Lemme help you out. You thought you'd given me enough time to miss you, so you're here to soothe my little feelings hoping we can fall back into our same routine." I rolled my eyes and crumbled crackers into my soup.

"Kharynn, it's not like that. I love you—"

"Save it. I'm running on empty, Charles. I have nothing left to give you or anyone else, all the fucks I had ran out when you told me we were done. Oh yea, I saw Eden last week."

"My wife?"

"Yea. She was driving Uber. What did you do to that woman, Charles?"

"Kharynn, I told you I was leaving her, and I did. I don't know what she doing for money, but if you say she driving Uber, I'm taking her back to court for custody." He looked away as he rubbed his beard, lost in thought.

"Why would you do that?"

"Because she a bum, that's why," he spoke through gritted teeth. "She been living off the money I'm giving her for child support until this case is done and not using it for my kids!"

"How much do you give her?"

"Look, I make sure her $520 is deposited in her account once a month! She had to move out of the house I'm paying for, if anything she should be glad I let her keep the car! Eden ain't never been nothing for as long as I've known her, she always been a bum!"

"What? I'm sure she was in that house making it a home for you and your kids—"

"Even before the kids, she ain't do nothing! I take that back, she used to work, was a lil' manager at her job for a while." He stood up and began pacing back and forth. "That was alright at first. Then when she got pregnant, she made me the happiest man in the world, and I told her that. Instead of her agreeing with me like a wife should, she told me she wanted to have an abortion. Said she wanted to stay on her job and work on getting promoted, not caring about my feelings, not caring about me wanting to be a father. I begged her…she had me on my knees begging her selfish ass to have my babies!"

"Ok, so obviously she had the girls. What's the problem?"

"She started acting like she was supposed to. I think it was because they cut her open when she had my girls. Thought she was gonna put them on formula 'cause she was too lazy to breastfeed. Talking 'bout how my babies always wanted to eat at the same time and her nipples were cracking."

"Did you at least take her feelings into consideration?"

"Women in Africa breastfeed twins just fine, I didn't see what the problem was. Do that even happen?"

"Do you have nipples?"

"Naw."

"Because all women aren't alike."

"Well I asked my aunt and she said she ain't never heard of nipples cracking! She should know, she got twelve kids and breastfed all of them. Like I said before, she just lazy!"

"You can't be serious right now, Charles." I rubbed my temples as they started to throb. "There's nothing that your aunt can tell you about your wife's nipples unless she's examined her personally."

"So, she went back to work after those six weeks," he purposely ignored me. "Thought she was gonna take more time off, said something about some extra weeks so she could 'bond with my babies'," he air quoted. "Trying to lie to those people after doing all that to keep that job. Then she started acting like I was asking for too much because I told her that just because she worked didn't mean nothing; she still needed to keep my house clean. Talking 'bout she needed a maid or a nanny when it wasn't nothing wrong with her two hands!"

"But if she worked, and you worked…"

"That money was going towards the house, not for her to sit around on her ass watching TV and doing nothing after she got off work!" he fumed. "Don't no man wanna work four days straight on a job to come home to a sandwich and a glass of damn fruit punch!"

"Hold on. If I'm hearing you correctly, she also worked a full-time job, washed and folded clothes, vacuumed, scrubbed toilets, dusted, took your babies that you begged for to and from daycare since you're a pilot…and on top of that she needed to also cook you a full meal plus wash dishes?"

"That's what a woman supposed to do! If I'm taking care of home—"

"The devil is a liar! She was the one taking care of home!"

"Either way, she quit that job to take care of my babies full time. That was selfish of her, she ain't ask me how that would affect me!"

"Did you care?"

"Anyway, that's when she really got lazy—"

"Lazy how?"

"I don't know, she just was!" he roared. "Like my mama said: women are the backbone of the home, she was supposed to do that! I'm the provider, what I look like washing some dishes or changing a pamper?"

I see your mama just as stupid as you, I thought, watching his tirade.

"That's why we couldn't be together no more—" he shook his head pathetically. "You know what I wish?"

The more he talked, the madder I got. "What?"

"I wish I would've had those babies with you. I love my daughters, I love them more than anything in the world, but their mother—"

"That's the life you want for me, Charles? That's why you over here checking on me?"

"Kharynn, everything's gonna be different with you!"

"Different how? You got that poor woman out here driving Uber, endangering her life to take care of her babies while you say $520 a month is enough for her to provide for a set of twins? That don't even cover her rent!"

"She live with her sister, you know she ain't charging her no rent—"

I stood up and walked to the front door, yanking it open so he didn't have a reason to keep talking. "Bye Charles."

"Now wait, hold on now, let's talk about this. You not Eden, you know how to go to work and—"

I felt a strange tingling in my gums as rage began bubbling in my stomach, bile slowly rose in my throat. "Charles you have to go now."

"Kharynn, I ain't going nowhere until—"

"LEAVE MY HOUSE BEFORE I CALL THE POLICE!"

"You crazy, Kharynn!" he stormed to where I stood just inside the threshold, trying my best to control the urge to suck the life out of this man. Eden would be a lot better off if he was dead. "I don't know what I ever saw in you!"

"You don't know what you saw in me? YOU DON'T KNOW WHAT YOU SAW IN ME, CHARLES? I don't know what I saw in YOU!"

"Bitch please, I gave you some of the best dick you ever had in your life!" he shot back.

"The best dick in my life?" I laughed. "Please! Compared to what I'm getting now, man you SUCK! You can't have weak dick and be an asshole, Charles! Pick a struggle!"

"Fuck you Kharynn! I was NEVER leaving my wife for you!" his voice echoed through the apartment complex. I knew my neighbors were outside being nosy.

"Fuck me, Charles? FUCK YOU!"

"YOU FIRST!"

"AAAHHH! GET OUT!"

I felt the sweat pouring down my face, and it wasn't from my illness. It was two o'clock in the afternoon on a sunny day in Georgia, but all I saw was the darkness. My tongue flickered subtly across my lowered incisors, the exotic electricity traveled through my veins…willing me to submerge my pointed teeth into his throbbing vein and free the world from this conceited egomaniac. Someone needed to save this man from me…somebody needed to get him away from me…

"I'm gone, you crazy bitch! And don't call me no more!" I heard faintly from the light. As he put space between me and him, my heightened senses began to subside. A gentle breeze cooled the sweat from my forehead while the brightness traveled closer to return my vision. The lump in my throat melted away as my stomach settled itself. I saw Charles's Lexus creep slowly through the parking lot and went back inside to soothe my aching emotions.

Nobody called you in the first place. Any small piece of love I thought I might've had towards him was gone when Vasilios sunk his teeth in my neck.

*

I was going crazy sitting in that house but scared to go outside for fear of what might happen. What if I walked into the store and somebody looked at me the wrong way? Would I pounce on them to take their life? Or what if I was driving and someone cut me off on purpose? Would they be a victim of my extreme road rage? More importantly, a voice in the back of my head kept telling me to go to Charles's house and strangle him dead. Regardless of how I felt about me and him, I was too cute to go to prison. And if I got life, who knows how long I'd be behind bars?

For the most part, my moods were temperamental, but with this new blood flowing through my veins, I didn't know what would set me off. Deciding to get out and smell some fresh air, I walked down to the mailbox, waving at one of my neighbors fastening her baby into a car seat. Flipping through the flat paper containers, I shuffled through bank statements and advertisements until my eyes landed on three envelopes with no return address, my name handwritten in Old English. *Vasilios.*

I debated tossing them in the trash and decided against it. Part of me longed to be with him, even if it was something as small as reading his words. I was beginning to wonder if my illness was from the change or because I needed him next to me.

Trudging back up the steps to my apartment, I laid the envelopes on the end table and started cleaning up. Charles was right, my house was a mess. Finally placing the last dish in the dishwasher three hours later, I took a quick shower and sprayed on his favorite scent. Vasilios loved the smell of sandalwood mixed with my natural pheromones; each time I sprayed on a certain perfume he'd eye me like I was a piece of that Wagyu steak he introduced me to on our first date.

Dressed in my bra and panties, I fluffed the couch pillows and got comfortable. I picked up the first letter and opened it, skimming the words on the page written with his hand:

Kharynn,

Out of body. That's how you make me feel. Out of sight, but never off my mind. We're not perfect, but every day you aren't in my airspace, I wonder why. Why I can't touch your skin, why can't I bask in your essence? Why you aren't here with me, letting me take care of you while you go through this process. The singular thought in my head since we met has been about how much I want us to grow as a couple, as a family, you as my wife. That day you gave yourself to me, all I wanted to do was to love you, protect you, provide for you, lead you and nurture you. I'm ready to begin my journey of forever with you…you are the calm to my storm. You complete me. If I have to write you a letter every day until you come home, then so be it.

I love you.

V.

"Is he serious?" I tried to swallow the lump that formed in my throat. I ran my fingers across the ink on the envelope before I opened it because I knew his hand had been there. Something that he'd touched, something…even if that something was the pen and paper, I needed to touch and feel his soul:

Kharynn,

You deserve a man that shows you he's everything you need without you telling him what you need. You are my queen. And as your king, I know you what you need right now. You need me to push your knees up and enter your secret garden head first. Once you provide me with the paint to work with, I'm gonna use my tongue as your brush to paint rainbows across each flower in your garden. When you start to feel the sun peek over the horizon, I'm sliding further down to your innermost chambers using that secret key to unlock your soul from that protected area. Only one king can do that for you baby: me. Then once the sun has arisen and your soul is free, I'm gonna straighten your crown so you can take your place by my side.

I miss you Kharynn. Come home.

V.

"I miss you too," I sniffed. Grabbing the third envelope, I snatched it open to see what message he had for me:

Mrs. Bello,

You know what my favorite memory is of us? The way you laughed at the look on the waiter's face at Spago when you asked him how to pronounce that dessert. At that moment, seeing the smile on your face...that's when I realized the depth of my love for you. I want to see that smile every day for the rest of my days. I'm ready for us to take more trips. I'm ready to make a big deal over your birthday. I'm ready to give you massages because that's what you deserve. Yes, my love, I was wrong. But I promise if you'll have me, I'll never fumble your heart again.

I love you,

V.

The ink on the paper smeared from the rivers of tears rolling down my face, pooling in tiny blobs dotted across the parchment. This man loved me unconditionally and completely with no strings attached. Every step of the way I compared us to my relationship with Charles when the truth was: they were nothing alike. "VASILIOS!"

Kharynn, he whispered in my ear. *Say you'll never leave me.*

I'll never leave you, Vasilios.

Say you'll never go…

I'll never go, my love.

I love you so much, he echoed, materializing next to me.

"I love you too."

Chapter 11

Vasilios

I hadn't laid eyes on her in almost a week, but the fire we made afterward was explosive; we made love the rest of the day and into the night. In the stillness of the dark was where we created the magic that came with being immortal beings; our moans could be heard by the cars intermittently swooshing by on the street. In the gyration of her hips, I felt the ebb and flow of the moon's natural tides; in her hypnotic movements, I became trapped between her svelte thighs. And when she submitted to my ethereal whims, I pollinated the honeycomb to nourish her garden amid her multiple releases.

"What can I do to make you happy again, my love?" I questioned, dragging my tongue down her body. I loved this woman's scent, when her pheromones mixed with the sandalwood splayed against her skin, she reminded me of my native Lagos.

"Mmm…thank you, Vasilios." She smiled sexily with her eyes still closed.

"No thanks needed, love." I allowed my lips to rest against her shoulder, watching her every move.

"But I'm still irritated. How do I know that this is the only thing you've been keeping from me?" she fumed, rolling onto her back.

"I swear…"

"You said that before, yet here we are," she interrupted with a finger to my lips. "I'm sorry. Vasilios I love you, but I can't tell you how to fix this. You're a man who has lived over lifetimes, I think anyone who can not only read minds but also respond should be able to figure this out. Please leave."

"Leave? Kharynn let's…"

"Conversation won't fix us, actions will. Thanks again, I feel so much better now." She smirked, slowly levitating towards the bathroom. "Oop, wasn't ready for that one!" she giggled.

"You levitate? When did that start?"

"I don't know, but I like it," she beamed. "One day next week we should meet up and discuss what I can and can't do. Right now, I need to sort out my feelings, so you can exit the same way you entered. See you later, babe."

"Kharynn."

"I said bye, Bello." She slammed the door to the bathroom, and I took that as my dismissal. Disappearing from my side of her very comfortable bed, I transported back to my condo, alone once more. Kharynn's apartment was small, yet cozy. She didn't have half of the trinkets I collected over the years; I could probably fit her whole apartment in my bedroom. In the opaqueness of my space, I became overwhelmed. My riches and antiques no longer mattered, what mattered was her. *Kharynn.*

Heading to the bathroom, I took a shower and towel dried myself off; thoughts of her floating in and out of my mental. To see her levitating was new for me and her; I didn't levitate. I never levitated. The sad part was, there was no one I could call to ask why her energy was different from mine. Kharynn was evolving and if that was the case, I had no advice to give her.

Moisturizing my skin with baobab oil, I pulled on a pair of underwear and opened the blinds. I preferred the humid Georgia air mixed with the smell of pine trees and cut grass to the artificial humidifier attached to the air conditioning piping through the building's walls. Staring blankly out over state road Georgia 400, I racked my brain thinking of ways I could make up my betrayal when my phone rang. Padding softly to where it sat on the mahogany wood wardrobe that I took from a slaveowner's personal stolen collection, I slid the button to the right and put the phone on speaker.

"Yeah."

"Vasilios, I don't appreciate being fired because I'm pregnant," Cyndi spat in my ear.

"You weren't fired because of your condition, we released you from Bello Enterprises because of your work performance."

"My work performance?" she gasped dramatically. "What was wrong with my work performance?"

"That's the real reason I sent you to work with Owen," I revealed. "I didn't want my assessment of you to be biased, so I sent you down the hall. When he told me that you weren't working out, I decided to terminate your employment."

"Without talking to me, Vasilios? Without giving me a chance to fix it?"

"Cyndi, we wrote you up three times! Your yearly assessment has been the same for the past two years: needs improvement. I'm confused as to why you're surprised! And how would I have known you were pregnant in the first place?"

"Because I called and told you it's yours!" she yelled accusingly. "I don't understand why you find it so hard to believe we made a child!"

"Cyndi…for the hundredth time I told you I—" my words caught in my throat when Kharynn crossed my mind, but not for the obvious reasons. "Is anything…has anything happened to you out of the ordinary?"

"I've been throwing up like crazy—,"

"No," I squinted, rubbing the space between my eyes, "…not anything hu—regular symptoms. I mean something that maybe isn't in a book or online about pregnancy symptoms…"

"Vasilios, I am pregnant with your—"

"Cyndi let me call you back," I rushed, disconnecting the call before she could reply. Rubbing my beard, I sat on the edge of the bed and went over a few things in my head. Was that—was that why she was levitating? Was I bearing witness to the actual conception date of my first child? I had to think back to when Mary first told me she was pregnant with the child I lost so long ago...

"I 'clare, I ain't neva seent nothin' like it," Wilbur and I plucked the white puffy balls from the green stalks at the same time. "That gal don' filled up three burlap sacks full'a cotton all by ha'self an' workin' on two mo' (That girl done filled up three burlap sacks full of cotton all by herself and working on two more)!"

"Yea, she got us out hea'(here) lookin' bad, don' she?" I replied, marveling at her slim body as she stood and stretched towards the radiant ball of light in the sky.

"An' that ain't the crazy part, Sil. Kno' what the crazy part is?"

"What the crazy part, 'Bur?"

"She jus' started doin' that tuhday. Yessidy she wuldn't workin' like dat (She just started doing that today. Yesterday she wasn't working like that)!"

"Is that right?"

"Yup! Been hangin' round that ju-ju woman down in the delta. I betcha she done put a rut on ha' so she won't get beat," he

grumbled. "Used tuh be the slowes' lil' thang out'chea, now she got all that screnght (Used to be the slowest little thing out here, now she got all that strength)! Whea' she git' that from ova-nite (Where she get that from overnight), huh?"

"Ova-nite, huh," I continued to watch her bent at the waist tending to her work. Mary may have been hanging around the ju-ju woman, but she wasn't last night. "You thank dem spirits be workin' that quick (You think those spirits be working that quick)?"

"I knows dey do!" he whispered harshly. "See, my wife went down tah see the ju-ju woman looking fo' sumthin' to get massa to turn ha' loose when he be beatin' on ha' so hard (See, my wife went down to see the ju-ju woman looking for something to get massa to turn her loose when he be beating on her so hard). Ju-Ju gave ha' sumthin...massa turnt a blind eye to e'ry thang she do nih (Ju-Ju gave her something...massa turns a blind eye to everything she does now). I knows that spirit magic work!"

"Well if the ju-ju dat scrong (that strong), why come e'rybody don' go see ha?"

"Cuz' e'rybody don' wanna sell dey soul to da devil (Because everybody don't wanna sell their soul to the devil)," he continued to whisper lowly. "I tole ha' not ta' do it, but she said it was 'itha that or die (I told her not to do it, but she said it was either that or die). I ain' wanna be wit'out ha' so I gave ha' my 'mission (I ain't wanna be without her, so I gave her my permission)."

"Dat's a helluva choice, but if'un I had ta' make it, I prolly woulda' don' tha' same (That's a hell of a choice, but if I had to make it, I probably would have done the same)," I agreed, wondering where she got that extra strength.

Old Man Johnson had been licking his chops every time he came outside to 'check' and make sure his free labor hadn't run off. One thing he hadn't realized: I didn't belong to him. I didn't belong to anybody. Only reason I was there in the first place was because I'd caught Mary walking by herself one day at the creek and made my move. At the time I was looking for some warm legs to climb between, but I got a lot more than what I bargained for.

That first time at the creek, I admit I took advantage of her. I told her how beautiful she was, then told her I was sent by the foreman for us to make a baby. She was naïve, and that only made me want her more. My incisors tingled when I entered her and her hymen broke; as we made love, I knew she would crave my attention each time I visited. I went to see her again after me and Wilbur talked and didn't bother to ask whether or not she was pregnant, only focused on sharing my legacy with her womb. A few months later it was obvious she was with child and considering the circumstances, I knew it couldn't have been anyone else's but mine.

Once I found that out, I made sure she stayed out of the fields, her carrying my child was enough incentive for me to do both her work and mine. At night, I'd sneak out to other countries around the world, stealing workers to do her chore. Stashing her burlap

sacks in caves until it was time for the overseer to collect our work,
I'd done everything in my power to ensure I had a child. In the end...

"I gotta call her. She gotta take a test tonight." Throwing on a t-shirt and a pair of chino shorts, I grabbed the keys to my Audi R8 and took the elevator downstairs. Riding down Peachtree Road on a Friday night in the summer with the top down, I waved at every female who yelled in my direction to get my attention. At the end of the day, that was all they wanted themselves.

I pulled into her apartment complex and killed the engine. Stepping out of my vehicle, I leaned on the hood of my car and thought about what this meant for me…for us. She was my everything, I didn't need anything else as long as I had her in my corner. If she was pregnant with my child, me and Trina had to talk sooner than later.

"Slumming tonight, aren't we? This isn't Buckhead." Cyndi's voice came from behind me. "Hmph, who lives here?"

"Are you— are you following me?"

"Well I had to see what had your mind so occupied, so when I saw your car pull out of your building, I followed it," she rubbed up against my chest. "I can't risk something happening to the father of my child on a night in the city where they commit the most vicious crimes, now can I?"

"Cyndi, what are you talking about?"

"I saw on the news the other day where a man was robbed and shot at a gas station not too far from here," she continued. "As a matter of fact, I think it was somewhere around here."

"You do know there are millionaires in Chamblee, right? They have a Porsche dealership on the same strip as the Audi store I bought this car from. The police department is a few blocks from here; they post up at that QT gas station all night! It's rappers that live in this building, what 'crime' you think going on over here?'

"Oh. Maybe it was somewhere else then," she replied dismissively. "Since this area is so safe, let's go to that hotel we passed—"

"Cyndi, go…"

"Hotel, huh." My worst nightmare was slowly coming true as Kharynn materialized next to me. "Vasilios you seriously out here having a lover's spat with your bitch after you just left my bed?"

"Kharynn, baby I swear this is not what it looks like—"

"His BITCH?" Cyndi turned towards my bride with angry slits. "We were happy before YOU came along!"

"Happy? Tuh! This man laps my pussy like a thirsty lil' puppy every time I leave the office early, hunny! For the whole weekend, Friday afternoon through Sunday night! If that's the 'happy' you talking about, you right! He is absolutely blessed! How she taste, pooh?" she chuckled.

Her juices were still on my tongue, I knew exactly how she tasted. "Pussy sweet like peaches and cream." Kharynn knew what to say to have my already engorged erection trying to poke through my chinos. Sensing her anger had me on go; her yin matched my yang like a perfectly fitting puzzle piece.

"Vasilios, really? Knowing I'm carrying your…you know what. It's fine. It's fine. It's fine," she rubbed my face tenderly. "We can get past this sweetheart. Let's go home so we can discuss this privately, ok?"

"Yea, Vasilios, go talk to your baby muva," Kharynn agreed with this slut. "But when you're done, come home." She stared at me pointedly with her arms folded across her chest, no doubt her way of reminding me of my words to her.

"Cyndi I'm not—"

"Bye, y'all. Vasilios don't forget what I said." Kharynn gave me one last smirk before she became translucent, then disappeared completely.

"Where did she go?" Cyndi looked around, bewildered. "Seriously, she was just standing right here—"

"Listen. You need to get this through your skull. I'm not the father of your child. I'm not your boyfriend. We never had anything remotely—"

"Vasilios, stop it, ok! STOP IT! We're going home to settle this—"

Kharynn appeared again out of thin air, only this time she was in a different form. A COMPLETELY different form. "Didn't I tell you this man belongs to me?" Thin fingers with daggers for fingernails wrapped around Cyndi's throat and pulled her close; the two women stood nose to nose. "You want me to show you why he's MINE?" Her scream pushed my vehicle back three inches, echoing through the neighborhood as her canine teeth dropped into view.

"Baby go home. Let your man handle this, ok?" I snickered at Cyndi's shocked expression.

"Keep playing with me, Cyndi. Vasilios can't always be there to save you, especially now that I know what your fear smells like," she sniffed up and down Cyndi's face. "Wrap this up and get off my block." Kharynn's intense resting bitch face fixated on Cyndi with a piercing intensity, next thing I knew she was on the ground. "Handle this, Vasilios, or I will."

"I got it, my love. Cyndi get your ass up."

Chapter 12

Charles

Every woman in my life was acting like they'd lost their damn mind. I knew I had some good sex, but for Kharynn and Eden to treat me like this…they must've both been seeing somebody else. I was a damn good catch, they should've been happy I picked them in the first place. I had flocks of women at my beck and call all over the world, to be with me was a blessing in itself.

Although we had children together, Eden and I had only been together for six years. I met her on a flight from Fort Lauderdale, according to one of the flight attendants she cried from Florida to Georgia. After the other passengers deplaned, I noticed she was still sitting in her seat staring out the window looking every bit of confused:

"Excuse me miss. Do you know where you are?"

"I've just landed in the seventh gate of hell, right?" she chuckled humorlessly.

"Uhmm…is there anyone I can call to help you? Do you need medical attention?"

"My best friend?" she whispered under her breath. *"I go out of town to bury my mother and see pictures of him and my best friend getting married? When was he going to tell me?"*

"I usually don't do this, but let's uhhh...let's go talk, ok?"

"Lemme ask you this: are you married?"

"I haven't been blessed with the woman created for me just yet," I spoke truthfully. "But when God sees fit for us to meet, I guess I'll know."

"You 'guess'?"

"The devil sends temptation as a test of your faith. When God is satisfied that I've passed that test is when He'll send her to me."

"Oh, you go to church?"

"Every Sunday I'm in town. Which isn't often, but I keep this around my neck to remind me of His mercy and grace." I pulled the gold cross from around my neck that I'd picked up from a souvenir booth in one of these airports.

"I love a man who loves the Lord," she smiled through watery tears. "Had I made that choice to begin with I wouldn't be in this situation now."

I extended my hand to help her out of her seat, and her frail body leaned into me for strength. No words were said as we made our way to Qdoba and sat down. "Are you hungry? Do you want something to eat?"

"Not really." She fidgeted with her hands, nervously picking at her fingernails. "Oh my God, I don't even know your name."

"Charles. I guess you can say I drove you from Florida to Georgia, I was the pilot on the plane." I tried the corny joke route to see if it would elicit a smile.

"Aww, that's cute. Thank you for getting me here safe."

"No problem. What's your name if you don't mind me asking?"

"Eden."

"Like the garden?"

"Yea."

"Nice to meet you, Eden. Hey, we don't have to talk about your situation if you don't want to, we can sit and enjoy each other's company. I'm ok with that."

"He humiliated me, Charles. I felt so small, so stupid seeing the video of their first kiss when the preacher pronounced them husband and wife posted on her Facebook page," she trembled. "I didn't think anything of it when he didn't want to come with me to Fort Lauderdale, he and my mother never got along. Looking back, I think she didn't like him because she knew him for what he was. She always asked if I was still with that ol' devil every time we talked. And now…" she wiped her nose before breaking down again.

"Not all men are like that, Eden. You still got some good guys out here."

"Is it," she spat, sarcasm lacing her words. "That's what they all say. Then, as soon as we let our guard down, this happens."

"Don't take that hurt out on every man you meet, Eden. I'm not saying don't be mad, but we shouldn't have to pay for the next man's indiscretions. HE hurt you, not us."

"What?"

"You know, that's why 77% of relationships don't work out. It's always that one person bringing in baggage from their past into their present."

"How do you know that?"

"I told you: I got God on speed dial." That was a lie; I'd fallen asleep watching Steve Harvey talk show reruns all night at the hotel.

"Well, it's refreshing to finally meet a man who knows how to care for a woman's heart."

"Care for it and the woman who comes with it," I beamed, turning on the charm. "I'm not trying to rush you into anything, I think you to heal first. But at least let me be here to help you through the darkness."

"Thank you, Charles."

We've been together from that day until the last argument when I had to force her out of my house. I came home and the house was clean except for my daughters' rooms. Celine's room had toys all over the damn place and Chanelle took all the sheets off her bed and threw them on the floor. And to top it all off, all three of them were asleep in the same bed without a care in the world. My babies needed their rest, but I didn't know what Eden was thinking:

I walked into my bedroom and kicked her feet hanging off the bed. "Wake up. Eden, I said wake up!"

"Hmmm…" she rubbed her eyes, looking around for my babies. "Where…oh. Charles shhh. I just got them down for a nap, they've been running all—"

"You can't handle two kids? Damn, get up off your ass and do something sometimes!"

"Get up off my ass? Have you forgotten who used to run this household when you got suspended for messing with that flight attendant back before we got married?" With each word, she stabbed her finger in my chest to emphasize her point.

"You my wife, you—"

"Supposed to do that, Charles?" she chuckled bitterly. "I wasn't your wife then, but I've always held you down! Boy, if it wasn't for your mother and your old ass aunts, we might have had a shot at a decent marriage!"

"You just mad because you ain't at that job switching your ass around that store in those tight pants no more!" I roared. "Married women don't wear that shit!"

"And married men are faithful to their wives, but since your mammy and her miserable ass sisters told you otherwise, here we are!" she shot back viciously.

"Ain't nobody gotta tell me about you!" I clapped back. "Everybody knows what kind of deadbeat you are!"

"Everybody who? We don't run in the same circles!"

"Ain't nobody stupid—"

"BUT YOU, CHARLES! I HATE IT HERE!"

"You hate it here?" I chuckled darkly. "YOU HATE IT HERE! LEAVE THEN!"

That shut her up. Eden trembled in front of me with her mouth dropped open, speechless. "Leave?"

"Yeah, leave!"

"I'm not leaving! THIS IS OUR HOUSE!"

"THIS IS MY HOUSE, EDEN WHITLOW! AND I SAID GET OUT!"

"I'm calling the police—"

"And tell them what? All I have to tell them is I'm the breadwinner and you don't work! They gonna escort your ass right down to the sidewalk! GET OUT!"

She started towards the closet, but I stopped her. "Only with the clothes on your back! You ain't taking nothing out of here that I bought!"

"I contributed to this house too, dammit!"

"Three years ago! That money gone!"

"Why are you doing this to me?" she dropped to her knees first, then crumpled into a ball on the floor, sobbing. "Charles I've always been a good wife to you!"

"Because I don't think the woman I want to be with should have to keep hiding in the shadows. It's not fair to her!"

"Not fair to her? WHAT ABOUT ME, CHARLES! I'M YOUR WIFE!"

"Let's not make a big deal out of this." I helped her up first, then passed her the Louis Vuitton bag on the dresser. "Face it, the love has been gone out of our relationship for a while now. I'll make sure the girls are taken care of and you can keep your car, ok?"

"Charles, I—I still love you…" she stuttered. "We can fix this…you don't think we should go to therapy?"

"We're already past that point, Eden. Don't make this any harder than what it already is. Let me help you to the car since the girls are asleep."

"Do you love her?"

"What?"

"You heard me, dammit! I said do you love her!"

"I love her enough to divorce you!" I shot back. "Crying ain't gonna make me change my mind, wipe your damn face!"

"As long as we've been together..." she continued to weep, "you've never truly cared about me. You've never put me first. It was always 'my mama said', or 'my auntie said'. Even when you weren't quoting them verbatim, the things you'd say to me aren't what a man says to the woman he loves." She sniffed.

"Oh, so now I can't talk to my family?"

"Do they know about her?"

"Why would I tell my mama I got a girlfriend? That ain't her business!"

"Neither was our marriage, but that didn't stop you though, did it," she spoke quietly. "You know what hurts me the most, though?"

"What's that, Eden."

"What hurts me the most is that you've changed. You've changed for this woman. Your mother doesn't know about her, yet she was always advising you on what to say to me. That's all I've ever wanted from you, Charles. That and your heart. You came into this for your own selfish reasons and never gave me either."

"Eden, stop with that psychological mess you got from watching Dr. Phil—"

"No, I got it from the same place you did that day we met: Steve Harvey. You quoted that man verbatim at the airport that day. I let you take advantage of me when I was at a low point in my life and this is what I got for not putting me first."

"I'm putting you first now: first take the key to this house off your key ring and leave it on the dresser. Second: make sure my daughters have a roof over their heads tonight. I gotta fly out—"

She stared at me in disbelief for a few more seconds, then unhooked her key fob from the rest of her keychain. "Regardless of everything you've done to me, Charles, I loved you unconditionally, even when I didn't want to. We'll be gone before you leave."

I let her sister come over a few days after I got back to get some stuff for her and the kids. Truth be told, I was done sneaking around. I was ready for me and Kharynn to take our relationship to the next step. The day I checked her cloud and saw she was in Charleston, I seriously thought she'd picked up a shift. Then I remembered: I told John to furlough her. She needed to know what it was like to be down to your last dollar with no one to call on but me. She needed to see who really loved her, even more than she loved herself. Without her job to use as a safety net, she'd start to respect the hand that fed her.

How she got to Charleston, I had no clue. Then it hit me: she was with that muscle-headed brotha that I saw her with that one night. That was some bullshit; I did my part. I told her how I felt, and she thought she was gonna leave me? It wasn't that simple for either of us. Feelings were involved, time had been invested, money spent. Lies told; I put my wife out for Kharynn. After all that she thought she was gonna walk away into the sunset with some new man all happy? I didn't see it that way. I didn't see it that way at all.

*

I sat outside watching her apartment every day. I was waiting to see her pull up with that pointy-headed, muscle-bound dude. If they did, I had words for him and her. Sitting in my car for hours watching her building, I thought about everything we'd been through. How much I sacrificed for her and how ungrateful she was. Then when I saw that light turn on in her bedroom window, I tried to figure out how she slipped past me. Either way, it didn't matter, she was about to stop playing games. Luckily the women in my life schooled me early on how women always played games for attention.

I crossed the street and took the steps to her apartment two at a time. Just as I arrived, I saw some kid coming up behind me with one of those Postmates warming bags in his hand and his phone in the other. "Hey, Karen?"

"Kharynn, asshole. Gimme this food." I snatched the bag from his hand and sent him on his way. Knowing she'd open the door since she was already expecting her food, I checked to make sure my breath wasn't funky, then knocked on her door.

Her response to me that day wasn't what I expected, but it did confirm what I thought all along: she was crazy. What other reason could it be for her acting the way she was towards me? Threatening to call the police and putting me out of her apartment? Last time we were together, I was licking her vagina in the cockpit of the flight from Raleigh to Atlanta. Now this? It was just like my mama always said: black women are conditioned to act like men, therefore they don't have no respect for them. All these women were the same.

I was currently on my way to L.A. alone for vacation. Since me and Kharynn weren't getting back together anytime soon, I was ready to get out of the city. Once me and Eden's divorce was done, I might move west for a new start. Since she couldn't afford a lawyer, I convinced her that the settlement for $5,000 and child support was all she got out of the marriage since that was all she put in. She hadn't worked since my daughters were born, so she didn't need anything more than that.

"Attention passengers, we will be landing in Los Angeles in approximately fifteen minutes. Local time is 4:15 p.m. and sunny skies for miles. Thank you for flying Delta!"

I let the seat tray up and handed the flight attendant my trash. Delta had some pretty decent flights, considering. They wouldn't let me go into the cockpit because although I was a pilot, I didn't work for their airlines. Which I understood to a point, but what if something happened and they needed somebody to fly this damn plane?

The descent and landing weren't bad, a little bumpy, but I was sidetracked by the hazel colored beauty in the seat across the aisle. She put me in the mind of both my ex-wife and supposed-to-be fiancé; if Eden and Kharynn were sisters this woman could pass for their cousin. New city, new possibilities.

"Excuse me, you dropped your Air Pods." I tapped her shoulder and pointed at her pretty feet with the gold polish.

"Oh, thank you! I don't know what I would've done if I would've got off the plane and didn't have them." We just met, but her smile already had me mesmerized. "Hi, I'm Lisa, and you are?"

"Charles." I held my hand out for her to shake. "What brings you to L.A.?"

"How about we talk about it over dinner at Chow's tonight?" she beamed, grabbing her phone from her bag. "What's your number, love?"

We exchanged numbers and walked through the airport for a while together before she said she had to go. I went back to the baggage claim area where we'd already passed my chauffeur who would be taking me to the Four Seasons for my stay. "You looking for Charles Whitlow? That's me. Grab my luggage and let's go."

*

The plan was to have Lisa's legs wrapped around my neck no more than an hour after we left Chow's, and that was with traffic. I was piping her down tonight so I had a reason to come back and forth out here to visit. Who knows, maybe she could slide into Kharynn's vacant spot.

I was in the bathroom lining up my beard with a straight razor when I heard a noise in the living room. "Hey, this room is occupied!"

"I know it is, why you think I came?"

"Kharynn?"

"Yep, it's me," I was beyond shocked when she strode into the bathroom where I stood. "How you doing today, baby?"

"I'm doing good…" I groaned, fondling her curves. "Wait, how you get here?"

"Asked around for a while at the airport." Lust oozed from her lips as she ran her hand across the black latex covering her triple D cups. "I still have a few friends up there."

"Mphf, they told you where to find big daddy, huh," I ran my fingers through her short brown tresses and breathed in her ear. "You miss me?"

"Mmhmm…"

I shoved my tongue between her lips, tilting her head back to savor her lusciousness. Kharynn pulled me in closer to devour my mouth, but there was a roughness to her actions. She seemed a little TOO eager, I felt like she was gonna pull my tongue out with her teeth. "Slow down baby, we got all night."

She stopped suddenly, taking a few steps back she cocked her head with a look in her eye that I hadn't seen before. "Don't you miss me, Charles?"

"Yea baby, I miss you, I'm just saying—"

"Charles, you don't miss what we used to do in the cockpit?" I watched her hand travel across her body and settle between her thighs. "I miss you."

"Kharynn—"

She bent over the back of the couch with her ass tooted up high in the air. "Spank me, Charles. Mmm…I've been a bad girl…"

"Got dammit, Kharynn that ass fat than a muthafu—what you been eating?" I smacked her generous lower cheeks and stood back to watch the waves crash against her thighs.

"Mmm…harder, Charles! HARDER!"

As I raised my hand in the air for a second time, a crushing hand wrapped around my wrist, snapping bones as the vice gripped my arm. "The hell is wrong with you beating on my wife!"

"AAAHHH! Your—what the hell is going on! Kharynn, you set me up!"

Her head jerked in my direction; heavily hooded lids concealed blood-red eyes glaring at me with pure malice. Deep-set wrinkles streaked across its face leading down to a pointed chin jutted outward in my direction. My mouth dropped open in shock; the woman twerking on the hotel's couch wasn't Kharynn. It wasn't a woman at all—

"Vasilios, I told you I'd get you back for that bitch Cyndi, didn't I?" the first thing mimicked Kharynn's voice perfectly, its' voice oozed seductress as it walked towards me with a provocative bounce in each step.

"Be gentle baby, you don't want to get sick from your first kill," the second thing gripping my wrist growled in my ear, cackling along with the first one. "Like your friend Charles said; take your time, we got all night."

"Please…please let me go! I got a wife and kids—"

"Ah, that's right. Your divorce isn't final yet," the one that looked like Kharynn—hold on…

"Please, I—I promise I won't tell nobody about anything that went on here, please let me go!" I cried real tears, scared to death. Was this how my life would end? Stuck in a room with these two— things? Monsters? No way out, my kids growing up without their father?

"Monsters only exist in the fairy tales of children to keep them up at night," the male thing hissed in my ear.

"Charles, Eden and the girls are going to be so much better off without you—" the female thing hissed eerily before it pounced on my neck...

Chapter 13

Cyndi

Kharynn thought she was gonna get rid of me that easy? Who knows what kind of lies she told Vasilios to get him to look twice at her ugly ass. It wasn't a secret that Black men with power preferred Caucasian women. We were prettier, we were smarter, and we knew how to take care of their needs. If they would just submit to their men, maybe they could hold on to them.

I grew up in Woodstock, Georgia, just north of Atlanta in Cherokee County. Not only was I prom queen in high school, I was also captain of the cheer squad, editor of the school newspaper, president of the yearbook committee and graduated valedictorian. Two years into my degree at Kennesaw State, I dropped out when my parents died in a car crash on I-75. To deal with that pain, I started having a glass of wine with dinner which quickly escalated to three bottles of alcohol a day. I knew I hit rock bottom when I rolled out of bed and showed up to my then-job at Heisenberg and Furst Law Firm still in my pajamas.

My aunt checked me into an inpatient rehabilitation center for alcoholics that same day. While on the road to recovery, I got a message at the facility that she'd died in her sleep. She was my last living relative that I knew of, which I took as a sign that I needed to get my life together. I committed myself to get better so I could live the long life that my family didn't. Landing the job at Bello Enterprises a few years ago was the icing on the proverbial cake.

When I first laid eyes on Vasilios Bello, president and CEO of Bello Enterprises, I was taken aback. Power exuded through his occasional glances; diplomacy fell in step along with the long strides he took. Even the cadence of his voice commanded attention and submission to his requests. I was in love.

For the first year and a half, that love wasn't reciprocated. Vasilios treated me like I was his employee; giving orders and demands, having his staff talk to me about my work performance. None of that would matter once I got him in my bed, so I ignored their suggestions. It was only a matter of time before he recognized me for who I was: the woman who deserved the right to be by his side as a man of power.

That night I spotted him at the club, I knew I had my chance. As his secretary, I had access to his work calendar and his cloud, he'd synced everything in one place for convenience. I made sure he still had the Find My app active on his iPhone and would track him all over the city. That's how I knew where he lived, he'd left his phone unlocked while he disappeared off to God knows where. He did that often, so I kept tabs on where he went and what he was doing.

When I saw him taking the same route I took to my favorite club down the street from my house, I knew it was fate smiling down on me. I found the sexiest blouse in my closet and paired it with a short skirt. Sending out a group text as I straightened my hair flat, I smeared on some nude lipstick while debating on whether or not to wear a bra.

I told my girls the plan while we were in the parking lot at the club. They would only walk in with me to make it look like me bumping into him was a coincidence, otherwise it would look more like what it was: me putting myself out there front and center so he'd see what he was missing. It worked, he took me to the hotel and I had to pull out every trick in the book to get my man. But I did. We both made promises to each other during that night of passion: he told me he could see himself with me for the long term when I wrapped my lips around his stiffness. He told me he loved me when he grabbed the back of my head and splashed his essence across my lips. He told me I was the only woman he cared about when he slipped his penis in my back door. And I knew from the way he said it, he meant it.

Seeing Kharynn walk into Bello Enterprises that day, I knew she was up to something. The way she strode arrogantly into his office with that patronizing smirk, I knew she'd be a problem. And I was right, she'd conned her way right into my position at Bello Enterprises. But I'd be damned if she also took his heart from me.

Ever since she'd been in the office, I noticed she'd start sneaking off for whatever reason. I tried to check her desk to see if I could find anything to use against her, but she locked up her paperwork whenever she left, even if it was to use the bathroom. Owen eyed me like a hawk; anytime he heard me moving around the office he wanted to know where I was going and what I was doing. The work he gave me I would finish in under an hour, then he'd send an email for me to complete another menial task. Vasilios wasn't like that, I had space in his office to work in the event I needed to take notes on a conference call or talk to a vendor.

When Trina called me in her office that Monday morning, I was under the impression that I would go back to being Vasilios's assistant while Kharynn dealt with Owen. After she explained why I was being fired, she gave me the number for an insurance company to receive my severance pay. Once I digitally signed the form they sent to complete my termination, I received a check for fifty thousand dollars. Not too bad for someone who was about to be married to a billionaire.

I blew through that money in two days. Now it was time for me to go get the man who I'd wake up next to for the rest of my life. And if I had to go through Kharynn for him, then so be it.

*

It took a lot of convincing at the airport, but when the plane landed in Los Angeles, I made it up in my mind that I wasn't leaving unless I was by his side. "One day, when we're both old and watching our grandchildren run around the house, me and Vasilios are gonna look back on all this and laugh," I mumbled, clacking my heels through the airport while calling an Uber to take me to the address on his phone.

I checked my GPS and saw he was somewhere in Beverly Hills. I didn't see an appointment on his calendar that said anything about he'd be out of town, much less in L.A. Nine times out of ten Kharynn lured him out here for whatever they called themselves doing behind my back. When she felt the need to make me aware of the fact that they were messing around that night, my heart dropped in my chest. Vasilios knew he wanted me; he just needed a little help seeing how good I was for him.

It had been a few months since we'd spent that time together, so I told him I was pregnant. As blessed as he was between his thighs, he shouldn't be surprised that the condom potentially broke, although it hadn't. Once I got him where I wanted him, I'd fake a miscarriage, which would only bring us closer together. Then he would wrap me up in his arms every night as we sobbed together for the loss of our baby, he'd ask if we could make love to me and after I—

"Hey, uhmm, this is your stop," the Uber driver called out over my thoughts. "You know, you're right around the corner from Rodeo if you like—"

"This isn't that kind of trip," I interrupted his spiel. "I appreciate it though!" I thanked him and left a tip on the app before I got out. Rolling the kinks out of my neck, I found myself standing in front of one of the most exclusive hotels in the area: the Beverly Hills Hotel. So many movies were filmed here…and so many celebrities also died here. Was that it? Was—was Vasilios so distraught over the last time we saw each other that he was coming here to—I had to save him.

With a heightened sense of urgency, I rushed to the front desk and cut the line. "Ahem, excuse me," a male voice called out from behind me. "I believe the line starts back there."

"Sir, my apologies, but I tracked my fiancé here to this hotel and I think he's going to do something terrible!" I wept.

"Honey, if he's cheating on you, there's nothing you can do about it," the woman standing next to him soothed like a mother figure. "You're a beautiful woman, go find someone who's going to love you for who you are and forget about him."

"No, no not that. See, he's been feeling depressed lately after we had this big fight and—"

"Oh my God! Last thing we need here is another scandal, we've never really got over that whole Whitney Houston thing!" the front desk clerk snapped to attention. "What's his name?"

"Bello. Vasilios Bello."

"Hmm…" Time stood still as her nails clacked across the keyboard, flipping through their current listing of visitors.

"Bello…Bello…here he is. Bungalow 8. Take this door out and hang a—"

"No, no, no, no, no, I need someone to escort me there. I don't know whether he's—" I trembled.

"Wait…wait, his booking is a double occupancy—"

"A double occupancy?" My lungs felt as if they were being weighed down by boulders, he was here with someone else? "A DOUBLE OCCUPANCY!"

"Listen honey," the older lady dug in her purse and pulled out a card. "Go see my shaman, he's the best in the world. Usually you have to have an appointment, just tell him I sent you and it's an emergency. A little green juice mixed with a little peyote and you'll forget this even happened."

"Who is she? Huh? WHO IS SHE!"

"Miss, we're going to need you to calm down—"

"No, dammit! I need to see him now! I'M HIS FIANCE!"

"What's going on here?" an older man stepped up to the desk, surveying the guests. "How can we be of service to you, miss?"

"Sir," I took a deep breath in and smoothed my hand down my dress. "I tracked my fiancé here to this hotel. He's depressed and suicidal and left his medication at home. I need to see him right now before he does something tragic, and this woman won't give me a key to his room!"

"Wha—that's not what happened, Sydney…"

"What happened to the customer always being right?" I fumed. "I saw this place has some pretty good reviews on Google, would be a shame if that five-star rating dropped because of a simple misunderstanding." I folded my arms across my chest and waited.

"Deilia, get Ms.—"

"MRS. Bello."

"Right," he gave me a condescending smirk. "Get Mrs. Bello a key to bungalow…" he checked the screen briefly to confirm…"8. Bungalow 8."

"Of course," she rolled her eyes while digging through a drawer full of keys.

"No key card?" I smirked. "I thought this was a high-end hotel!"

Sydney gave me one last tight smile and walked away. The couple behind me snickered for a second, whispering in quiet undertones. "Miss, if you must know, this is THE Beverly Hills Hotel. Hotels that are more…" she stopped to clear her throat, "…economical," I felt my face flush at her insinuation, "have key cards. Our guests pay for anonymity as well as privacy. You're standing inside of a hotel that has hosted Hollywood royalty, of course we wouldn't blemish our legacy with something so cheap as a key card," she sneered with an air of superiority. "Now if you wanna take this hall and make a right, you'll find yourself on the other side of the grounds where the bungalows are, follow the signs until you see the number 8. That's the number AFTER 7. Have a great day!"

"Uhmm, excuse me—"

"Miss, please," she shooed me to the side and waved the next customer over. "You're holding up the line. Have a great day."

The couple that was so nice to me a few minutes ago shoved me aside as they stepped up to the desk to be helped. Seething with anger, I kept my composure long enough to follow her directions. Walking through the hotel with its expensive mid-century modern décor, I thought about her words. Deilia said Hollywood royalty had walked these grounds, maybe when Vasilios got himself together and ditched his little friend, we could go see some more sights like the Hollywood sign or stroll on the Walk of Fame.

Winded when I finally found bungalow eight, I stopped for a few seconds to catch my breath, hearing the neighbor's dog growl on my right side. Out of nowhere, my stomach began doing backflips; a part of me didn't want to see who or what was on the other side of that door. Ignoring the voice in my head, I fished the key from my purse, taking note of how sweaty my palms were, and turned the knob.

Once my eyes adjusted to the darkness, I saw the room was decorated to his…OUR taste. Vasilios wasn't there, so I decided to sit down and wait for him and his 'occupant' to show up. "Yea, Kharynn is gonna blow a fucking gasket when she finds out he's out here with me," I giggled, running my hand across the suede couch.

"Ehhh…probably not a gasket. This whole 'Mrs. Bello' charade is funny though." Kharynn scared the living shit out of me when I heard her behind me because I knew there was nothing there but a wall.

Still trying my best to remain unbothered, I walked to the other side of the room and took a seat on the couch. "Give it up, Kharynn. Do you realize how big of a fool you're making out of yourself?"

"Nope. I don't. Why don't you explain it to me?" Her words dissolved into a devious grin. She was up to something.

"You know, I was initially going to let this whole thing play itself out so Vasilios can get you out of his system, but now…"

A light glimmered softly from her left side, casting an eerily bright ray against her face while leaving the other side in a shadowy shroud. "Now what, Cyndi?" she questioned, the cadence in her voice went from an alto to a deep bass in seconds, then back to alto. Fear clutched my chest like a tight fist; a breeze blew against the back of my neck when I realized as she approached that her feet weren't touching the floor.

"Uh…uh…now…I…I…uhmm…"

"No Cyndi, Vasilios is your man, right? Defend your man. Defend your relationship. If it were me, I would. Hit me, sweetie."

"I…I didn't…I didn't come here to fight you, Kharynn…"

"For a man like Vasilios, you wouldn't fight me?" she uttered curiously in my ear.

"What? No. Me Kharynn? No…no I wouldn't fight you. I think we can settle this like two—"

It happened so quick; I didn't have time to react before my skull fractured from the impact of her landing a closed fist to my face. "You don't know the kind of man Vasilios is, do you?" she let out the tiniest hint of a sneer. "The power that oozes off of that man every time I'm in his energy field…" Kharynn grabbed my neck and dangled my body high in the air her. "And the sex is amazing! Cyndi, have you ever made love to Vasilios?"

"Ye…yes," I croaked, moments from blacking out completely.

"Mmmm…has he ever stood in the middle of that massive condo, flipped you upside down, wrapped your legs around his neck and licked you from your pussy to your asshole with that long, thick tongue of his?"

"N…no."

"Has he ever sat you on his lap and stared in your eyes while he slipped two fingers between your thighs and watched your sex faces until you felt tears in your eyes? You wanted to open your mouth to beg him to stop and exploded cum all over his lap? Then he licked you off his fingers, stuck his tongue down ya throat and did it all over again?"

"No." I wheezed.

"Has he ever taken his fangs and dragged them over the full length of your body, purposely ticking your thighs with those pointy teeth?"

"Fangs?"

"Mmm…did he turn you too, Cyndi? Are you an immortal being like us?"

"Immortal being?"

"VASILIOOOOSSSS! Come to me NOW!" she screeched. Hairline cracks traveled the length of all four walls; plaster dropped from the ceiling at the vibration of her words.

"Yes, my love?"

If I hadn't seen it with my own two eyes, I'd swear someone was lying if they told me this man materialized out of thin air. But that's exactly what happened.

"Cyndi says she's not one of us. How is it that she's carrying your child and she's not one of us?"

"Because she's not carrying my child, my love." He kissed the back of her hand sweetly before setting his sights on me. "How did you get in this room?" he growled…the same growl I heard as I was walking up.

My face was pounding on one side from Kharynn's fist and I was struggling to catch my breath. "Oh, silly me. Gotta put you down, don't I?" she snickered.

"Kharynn, don't—" I pleaded to no avail, feeling the full brunt of the impact when my body crashed against the interior wall. "Why…why are you doing this to me?" I cried softly. "I haven't done anything to you!"

"You're right. The only thing you 'haven't' done to me is try to take my man," she circled my crumpled body, sniffing the air. "What me and him have, sis you could nevaaa…mmm…there it is. There it is. Can you feel it, Cyndi? Your fear…it's oozing from your pores…"

"That's enough Kharynn. We already had to toss Charles in a dumpster behind the swap meet," Vasilios warned. "Aren't you full?"

"Your son wants more, Vasilios. He needs more…"

"I knew you were carrying my child." He stood behind her and palmed her flat belly. "All the more reason why you need to stop this."

The more I watched as they proudly put their love on display for my benefit, the madder I got. I would've kicked that baby right out of her if I could move my leg.

"Do it, Cyndi." Kharynn's glare suddenly fixated on me once more. "You want me to help you raise your leg?"

"Kharynn, I—"

"Leave us, Vasilios."

"Kharynn—"

"I SAID LEAVE US! And get ready to pay a small fortune for the damage I'm about to cause in this room!" she roared before she snapped my ankle like a twig. "Hush little baby, don't say a word. Mama's gonna buy you a mockingbird. And if that mockingbird don't sing, Mama's gonna snap the neck of this bitch, Cyndi..."

Chapter 14

Kharynn

I don't know if me being in his airspace activated something in me, or how this whole thing went, but after we made up, I felt AMAZING. My level of unbotheredness was on one million and only went higher as time went on. That voice in my head that told me to strangle Charles…yea, I had to take her up on that one. I tortured Cyndi in that bungalow to the point that she begged me to kill her, so I did.

"Feel better now, love?" Vasilios reappeared from the shadows as I sat in the middle of the bungalow bathed in Cyndi's blood.

"I feel great!" I smiled like a kid in a candy shop. "How are you, my king?"

"Truthfully? I'm worried about you."

"Why, Vasilios?"

"Why? Kharynn, look at this room! You can't go around killing everybody who pisses you off! This—" he waved a hand over the room that I'd trashed, "…this is unacceptable. How are we supposed to explain this to anybody?"

"Vasilios, you are a billionaire—"

"And you have blood all over this room! In this day and age that's a safety hazard, Kharynn! Who cleaning this up!"

"Baby—"

"They might have to tear this whole bungalow down Kharynn!" He stopped yelling and took a seat on a chair that wasn't covered in blood. "Baby, I'm not mad at you, I'm mad at your actions. You can't be drawing attention to us like that, even now with the spiritual awakening going on in the world, people still don't believe there are actual vampires and werewolves out there. I got a lot to lose if people find out my true identity."

"You worried about your money and social status, Vasilios? Is that—"

"Kharynn, right now the only thing I'm worried about losing is YOU. Look at you, baby. You're covered in blood, got Cyndi's blood seeping into the cracks in the walls…this life might not be for you."

"No…at first I thought it wasn't, but now—"

"I'll find someone to clean this up. Like I said before, money isn't an issue. It's never been an issue. But if anything happens to you because of this—"

"Anything like what?"

"You showed Charles your true identity. You showed Cyndi your true identity. If you get mad, you can't be levitating around the city with your fangs dropped and red eyes!"

"Tuh! What somebody gonna do to me? I'M A FUCKING VAMPIRE!" I cheered.

"Kharynn, you know what would happen if someone tried to kill you?"

"You said I can't die—"

"I told you how people have tried to kill me, I never said you absolutely couldn't die," he schooled. "Just like I told you I've aged. I've been a vampire since I was sixteen years old, so I have a lot of knowledge about how this whole thing works. But I got that knowledge from experience; an experience that I gained from watching, listening and doing. Not from sucking on people's necks and drinking blood out of goblets."

"You mean to tell me you were born in the year 1676?" I questioned, still amazed at how good he looked for his age.

"Yes, I was."

"Were you a slave?"

"No one ever owned me, Kharynn. Other than you, that is." Vasilios chuckled. "Me and my mother came over from Lagos as free black people, we weren't a part of the trans-Atlantic slave trade.

I have to be honest with you though, you aren't the first woman who I have given my seed."

"See, that's what I'm talking about, you constantly—"

"Aht, aht, don't do that," he cut me off quick. "You never asked."

I rolled my eyes to the ceiling, he was right. "So how many kids you got then?" I kissed my teeth, waiting to see how many stepchildren I had and determine if I wanted to be bothered.
"None."

"But you just said—"

"I said you weren't the first woman I gave my seed. I didn't say I had children."

"Oh…Vasilios I'm so sorry," I covered my mouth with my hands. "I didn't know."

"He died in childbirth." Vasilios dropped his head and took a deep breath. "It was sometime around the 1800s, when Lincoln abolished that heinous act it wasn't as well-known as some of these school textbooks would lead you to believe. We didn't find out until the turn of the century, and even then, it wasn't completely removed from the law books in some states until recently. I say that to say this, love: I can't control people's attitudes around our kind. If anything happened to you, this country will be a wasteland until I take my last breath."

At that moment, I realized he needed me. Not physically, but he needed my love…he let me in to protect his heart. Yes, Vasilios had lived over multiple lifetimes, but I never asked how many times he'd been in love or lost someone near and dear to him. He needed me to protect his heart. "What happened to your mother?"

"I don't know exactly what happened, but the village elders burst into our home and dragged my mother out. Our neighbor's daughter was jealous of my mother's beauty, so she'd gone to the village and told them she saw my mother lighting candles and praying to the moon. Off the word of this one girl, they didn't have a trial, didn't follow any of the tests they put in place to prevent false accusations. They had her tied to a stake and wouldn't let me through the crowd, but her screams—" he stopped to take a deep breath in and exhaled, "her screams echoing through the treetops of the woods surrounding the town of Salem still haunt me to this day."

"Vasilios, I'm sorry—"

"Nothing for you to be sorry for, love. You weren't there."

"But you were."

"I'll be fine." He stood up and stepped quietly into the adjoining bedroom. Hearing the story of what happened to the one woman who loved him more than any other woman ever could broke my heart. I wanted to be there for him to comfort him.

"Babe, I know sometimes I'm not the best communicator," I rubbed his back as he continued to breathe deeply to keep his memories at bay. "But just like you've always been here for me, let me be here for you."

"Kharynn," his words were low and controlled. "I said I'm fine."

"Look at me, Vasilios."

"Gimme a—"

I grabbed his chin and tilted his face towards me; my heart broke seeing the tears that sat pooled in his eyes. "Men cry too, my love," I spoke softly, touching a finger to the wetness pooled in the hallows of his eyes. "You can't always be the strong one, it's ok to feel pain."

"Kharynn my love, when I tell you that you complete me, I mean that in every sense of the word, every phase of my life up to this point has prepared me to meet you," he whispered with my head cradled in his hands. "Do you know how much I love you, how much I cherish you? How I want to be with you for the rest of my days?"

"Considering I have a permanent reminder of your love on my neck, I think it's safe to say I have an idea," I giggled. "What can I do for you, my love? How can I make you feel better?"

"Make love to me," he uttered seductively, slipping his tongue between my lips.

Chapter 15

Vasilios

Eight blissful months with the woman I loved as my baby grew was all I've ever wanted out of life. Kharynn understood me better when we sat and talked about what I needed from her and she needed from me. We had sit-downs once a week when we sat and discussed us, a weekly check-in for our relationship. She thought it would be good for us to tell each other where we stood, how things were going communication-wise, what we could do to develop our relationship. We discussed our needs, our do's and don'ts. After a few weeks, we found that we both wanted the simpler things; walks in the park, Sundays at home, and enjoying each other's company. I loved going to her doctor's appointments to see my son as he grew bigger and stronger, ready to hold him in my arms and teach him how to ride a bike, change a tire, and most importantly, how to love a woman like his mother.

Every day when I came home from work without fail, Kharynn had my clothes laid out on the bed, dinner cooked, and CNN on the TV. I offered to get her some extra help around the house, but she said no, she could handle it. I loved how we were so in sync and the fact that I recognized her for who she was before I knew her name was crazy.

"Vasilios…" I smirked cockily every time I heard my name on her lips…those full lips that I'd done so many things to and had done so, so many dirty things to me… "Is that you, love?"

"It's me, babe." Upon stepping further inside, I saw her sitting on the couch in her bra and panties with a book in her hand. My baby loved to be comfortable. "What you over here reading, Dracula?" I leaned in and kissed her on her lips.

"No, I'm reading The Five Love Languages by Gary Chapman," she stuck her head back in the pages. "Have you read this yet?"

"Not yet. What's it about?"

"In a nutshell, it's a love manual for couples. There are five love archetypes that we all identify with, and how we love each other depends on those traits."

"So, what's your love language?"

"See, I would tell you, but—," she folded the book close to her chest, scooting to the other side of the couch, "then you won't read it."

"Ooohhh, I gotta read it too?" I placed her feet on my lap and started massaging her toes.

"Mmm…Vasilios, I'm serious babe…mmm…"

"Read it to me."

"You gotta stop massaging my feet first; I'm about to go to sleep," she rolled her head back and took deep breaths.

"You gonna tell me your love language?" I tickled her feet.

"Words of affirmation! Words of affirmation! Stop Vasilios!" she giggled with her nose scrunched up. "You play too much!"

"I should've known that," I tried to duck when she swung the book, but she caught me on the shoulder. "What's mine?"

"You, my love, yours is physical touch," she moved her face close to mine until our noses touched. "You love to touch and be touched. If we aren't in the same airspace, it drives you crazy; you get to twitching like a fiend."

"Lemme see this book." I slid the paperback from between her hands and perused a few pages. "We can read this together if you—what's wrong?"

Hee-hee-hoooo, hee-hee-hoooo… "Vasilios my water just broke…" *hee-hee-hoooo, hee-hee, hoooo…*

I glanced at the couch pillow underneath her and it was saturated. The panicked look in her eyes told me it was only a matter of time before my son made his appearance into this world, and I sprang into action. "Keep doing your breathing techniques like we learned in our birthing class, hee-hee-hoooo, hee-hee-hoooo," I breathed with her as I tore through the condo to grab a dress for her to throw on.

"Vasilios, call…call the ambulance…OOOUUUUCH!" she called out as another contraction knocked her on her ass.

"I called them while I was grabbing—"

"OOOWWW…I have a bag packed! Vasilios please…they won't get here in time! We have to—"

"Kharynn, they're on the—no baby, come back!" I yelled, watching her transparent figure as she tried to teleport to the hospital. "Kharynn!"

"Vasilios, I swear if they aren't here in the next—"

BAM! BAM! BAM!

"Baby, that's them, come back!" I didn't know how my son would respond to her using her mind to rearrange her atoms so she could reappear in a different location, and I didn't want to find out.

Kharynn's full shape came into view just as I opened the door to let the EMT's in. Helping her onto the stretcher, I followed closely behind, not letting her or my son out of my sight. We rode down the service elevator and they loaded her into the back of the ambulance, making room for me to climb in behind her and took off to Northside Hospital. "Breathe baby, just like we—"

"Shut the hell up, Vasilios! I'm not laying on this stretcher dead!"

Oh shit. "Baby, I just wanted to make sure you were—"

"I said shut the hell up Vasilios!" she screamed again, shattering the glass containers in the back of the ambulance. "If you wanna help, tell that fucking driver to get me to the—AAAHHH! GET THIS BABY OUT OF ME!"

"Ma'am we need you to calm—"

"BITCH I AM CALM!" she snapped, writhing in pain. "Vasilios, you are NEVER—AAAHHH!"

"Mrs. Bello—"

"I haven't married this asshole yet! He's never touching me—VASILIOS HELP ME!"

"Mr. Bello, we have to check and see if he's crowning," the female EMT rushed. "Her contractions are way too close together…"

"You mean she's going to give birth now?"

"Right here on Johnson Ferry Rd., because this traffic is not letting up," the driver called out. "Is everybody ok back there?"

"DOES EVERYBODY HAVE A HUMAN PUNCHING THEIR UTERUS OR IS IT JUST ME!" she screamed. "VASILIOS! DO SOMETHING, DAMMIT!"

"You heard her! Check her!" I was getting frustrated; she was yelling at me, the EMTs were looking at me like I'd done something, and a voice in my head told me my son was pissed because everyone was taking too long.

"I feel his head! Mr. Bello, we need you to help her push."

"Kharynn, I need you to breathe—"

"Vasilios, I'm so sorry, I'm so, so sorry, please baby, I love you—"

"Breathe, love. Like we did in class," I rushed. I was scared myself, but I had to be calm for her. "Hee-hee-hoooo, on the count of three, give me a big push, ok?"

"Ok, Vasilios, ok, please make it stop, please make it stop," she whined, nodding her head. "Hee-hee-hoooo AAAHHH!"

"The head is out! One more push!"

"Come on, Kharynn, one more, ok baby? Hee-hee…"

"AAAHHH!" we yelled together and with…our beautiful baby *girl*.

*

"Y'all gimme this lil' chocolate baby!" Maxine cooed softly to our daughter. Khamille Vivienne Bello was eight pounds and gorgeous. She had a head full of hair, my lips and nose with her mother's eyes, skin color and lungs. She already had me wrapped around her little stubby fingers and she wasn't even six hours old.

"Nah Max, you might have to get the next one, lil' gorgeous right here is all mine." I lifted my baby out of her hands and she wiggled herself comfortable in my arms, smiling to herself.

"Already a daddy's girl, I see," she smiled at both of us. "Kharynn, y'all was supposed to name her Maxine. We had an agreement!" she playfully tapped my fiancé on the shoulder.

"That's between you and Vasilios," she giggled with her friend. "See where she at now!"

"I'm just messing with y'all. Seriously, she is an adorable little girl."

"Thank you," me and Kharynn both spoke at the same time. "Come on now baby, you know I did the most work that night."

"So? I carried her!"

"And I thank you for that, but this little girl is her daddy's creation," I cooed to my daughter. "We can make another one after your six weeks are up."

"What? After all that pain you put me through? I got glass all in my hair and whatnot, I ain't having no more—" We all stopped to watch the door as it opened slowly and a head peeked in. "Can we help you?"

"Uhmm, my apologies if this is a bad time, but—"

"Eden? What are you doing here?"

Chapter 16

Kharynn

"I'm sorry, uhmm…have we met?" Eden slipped quietly inside as Vasilios looked back and forth between us, confused.

"Uhmm…yea…did you used to drive Uber?" I blinked, flustered. Eden Whitlow was the last person I expected to see in my private suite.

"Yea…but that was a while ago," she looked away with a slight frown. Charles had been gone for less than a year, and although he was an asshole, he was still her husband. "But uhmm, yes…I'm the registrar here at the hospital and we need to get your insurance information."

"Babe, we'll step out so you can take care of that," Vasilios laid Khamille in her bassinet and kissed my forehead. "I'll check up on you in a little bit. Maxine, let's go find the cafeteria, I'm starving."

"They have some pretty good food here," Maxine walked to the door with him. "You buying, right boss man?" I heard her say as they walked out.

"Your daughter is gorgeous," Eden smiled warmly. "Congratulations to you and your husband."

"We aren't married yet but thank you." Guilt gnawed at my stomach as I thought about the affair I had with her husband. Eden hadn't done anything to me. I knew Charles was married; he never hid that fact. Why would I purposely set out to hurt this woman?

"Not married? Oh, the EMT has your information listed as Kharynn Bello," she perused the paperwork Vasilios filled hastily scribbled on as we sat in traffic. "What's your last name, hun?"

"Lewis. Kharynn Lewis."

Eden started writing, then stopped, as if a light bulb went off in her head. "Kharynn Lewis. Why does your name sound so familiar?"

"I'm not sure."

"Lewis…Kharynn Lewis…do you work at Southwest Airlines?"

"I used to." Sweat beaded against my brow, but I wasn't telling on myself.

"I knew you looked familiar." She sat down in the chair next to the window and sighed. "You know, when I found out who you were, I went through all these different scenarios in my head on what I would do, what I would say to you."

"I'm lost," I lied. "What are you talking about?"

"My name is Eden Whitlow. Charles Whitlow was my husband."

"Charles Whitlow the pilot," I nodded. "Yes, I know your husband." No sense in denying it, she obviously knew who I was.

"If you're wondering, I found pictures of you and him on his phone after he died," she took a deep breath in and blew it out. "Pictures from all over the world, and he never took me any further than Lake Lanier."

"Eden, I'm so—"

"Did you know about me?"

"Excuse me?"

"I said did you know about me. Did my husband tell you he was married?"

"He did but—"

"There's a 'but'?" she spat lowly. "Where I'm from, women stick together, whether we know each other or not. The fact that my husband told you he was married, and you STILL fucked him makes YOU look bad! Not him!"

"Why not him, Eden? HE knew he was married before I did!" I shot back. "Now I'm not saying what I did was right, and I'm not saying you're wrong for feeling the way you do, but you can't place his cheating fully on my shoulders as if he was innocent!"

"Did you know he was leaving me for you?"

"Eden, I swear by the time I found out, Charles and I were already done."

"He tossed us out of the only home our children knew for you and I wanna know why! Is that… is that his baby?" she raged.

"Absolutely not!"

"But how—"

"Eden, I'm 1,000 percent sure this baby belongs to Vasilios Bello," I stopped her mid-sentence. "You have NOTHING to worry about there."

We both sat quietly for a second, lost in our thoughts. For me, I could finally close that chapter in my life where I spiraled into a pit of despair where I didn't even recognize myself. This moment in my life had been a long time coming, I broke this woman's heart. I damaged her spirit. This woman thought she wasn't worth the love her husband should have given her as his life partner because of me. The fact that he was long gone meant nothing; she was left to pick up the pieces of her life alone and by herself. I caused this woman hurt and she'd done nothing to me.

"I just don't understand why he would marry me knowing he didn't love me," she wept quietly. "In the beginning, I felt it, but when I found out he had gotten caught with one of the flight attendants…was that you?"

"No."

"He loved you, Kharynn." She stared out the window, dabbing at the corners of her eyes. "He told me he loved you. He didn't want us; we couldn't go to therapy because he loved you. I'm looking at you now, and although I want to hate you, I can see why. You're beautiful—"

"Eden, please don't do that."

"Do what?"

"Minimize who you are because of your husband's infidelity. YOU are beautiful. YOU are an amazing woman. This man broke you, yet you're still here. This man brought you to one of the lowest points in your life, yet you're still here. Taking care of your babies, doing what you must do to provide for your daughters. You're a strong and beautiful woman, Eden. I pray that one day someone comes along and showers every piece of you with so much love that there's no doubt in your mind of that fact."

Eden covered her face with her hands, her shoulders heaving up and down as she cried. I walked over to where she sat and put my arms around her neck as she wept. "Where do I go from here? What do I do? Who do I call? Charles is dead and my marriage has been over for a long time. When does the hurt stop?"

Her words tore me up inside, whoever said time heals all wounds couldn't have been speaking from experience. And she was right. Who could she call that would give her advice without reprimand? Where could she go to heal HER heart without feeling guilty for being selfish? When does her hurt stop? Or will it ever stop? Will she find the one man that was obsessed with her, in love with every piece of her mind, body, and soul?

"I can't answer any of those questions for you. All I can say is look deep within yourself in your quiet moments and reconnect with that person is that you should always love first. Nurture her. Tell her how much you care. Apologize to her for neglecting her, apologize to her for allowing others to hurt her. And do everything in your power to make sure she's loved, needed and cared for."

"Thank you, Kharynn," she sniffed, wiping her face. "Thank you so much. I forgive you."

"Eden, from the bottom of my heart, I am truly sorry. And I thank you for your forgiveness."

"Everything ok in here?" Vasilios stepped through the door with his left eyebrow raised.

"Yes, love we're good. Eden is Charles's wife. Eden, this is my fiancé, Vasilios." I introduced them although technically she and I were meeting for the first time today.

"Nice to meet you, Vasilios. I take it you're the one who loved Kharynn enough to see her worth," she smiled politely as she shook his hand.

"We helped each other see the good in us," he replied truthfully. "Listen, she told me about the relationship between you and her husband, and although I didn't know him personally, I apologize to you for the male species. We're all flawed, but all it takes is the one who is bonded to our soul to heal us from our past mistakes. I pray that you find that one and he loves you from the top of your head to the depths of your very being."

"Do you have a brother?" she blushed timidly. "Because if so—"

"Sorry, I don't," he chuckled as we all laughed together. "But trust me, the man for you is out there. Take care of yourself, Eden."

"You two are such a beautiful couple. I wish you all the best of love together!" she called out as she disappeared through the door.

"Hmm…how did that conversation go? I come back and you two are hugging?" Vasilios turned to me with a smile.

"She needed that. Charles messed her up bad." I nuzzled my head against his stomach. "Babe, you need to start back working out. Where did that come from?"

"What, my baby weight?" he chuckled, rubbing his hand across his little pudge. "Yesterday I was sexy, now I'm fat, huh."

"Whatever you are, you're my lil' fat daddy," I placed my hand atop of his as he leaned down to peck-kiss the top of my head.

"Ain't nothing little about me, you of all people know that VERY well," he moaned sexily in my ear. "When the doctor say I can clap them cheeks?"

"VASILIOS!" I gave him a playful shove. "You'll be the first to know when I find out."

A soft knock on the door broke both of us out of our nasty banter. "Who is it?"

"It's me, Vasilios," Trina eased in my room carrying a bouquet of pink and silver balloons along with two dozen roses. "Can I come in?"

"Of course, you can, we're family," I beamed. "Come see the baby."

Vasilios picked her up out of her bassinet while Trina washed her hands. "I can't believe you two had a baby. Did he tell you I told him to leave you alone?"

"What! Why?"

"I wanted mommy to take over my position at Bello Enterprises," she cooed to the baby while bouncing her up and down. "Which brings me to my next point: Bello, I'm resigning." She sang happily to Khamille.

"RESIGNING!" we both yelled at the same time. "Where are you going? Trina, what is the company going to do without you?" I questioned first.

"If it's about pay—" Vasilios started.

"No, it has nothing to do with pay," she laid the baby down in her bassinet. "I'm telling you both now so you can find a suitable replacement. And before you say you'll take care of it, Vasilios, I already posted my position to a couple of job boards as well as the company website."

"But Trina, why?" I felt like I was about to lose my best friend.

"Oh, Kharynn," her hand against my face felt familiar, but I was confused as to why. "It's time for me to go. Seeing you and Vasilios start your own family…that's always been my main goal."

"What?"

"Trina who—" Vasilios began.

She reached into Khamille's bassinet a second time, holding our daughter close to her heart, then lifted her up so that they were eye to eye. Khamille wiggled for a second before she opened her mouth to let out a long baby yawn. "Vasilios, the baby has fangs—"

"Just like her aunt." Trina smiled wide, revealing sharp, diamond encased incisors—

The End

Coming Soon

"Is this the address?"

"That's it."

I secured my hair back into a tight, low ponytail before pulling my helmet down over my head. "Let's do this."

The four-inch heels on my Gucci boots clacked angrily against the pavement as I moved from the building to my bike. My hand absently moved across my thighs before settling against the crevice of my honey pot. When I found out what was going on in the streets right under my nose, my mind told me that this job needed to be done by me and not my team. My tongue dragged slowly across my teeth and wet my bottom lip with anticipation. Nothing excited me more than putting in work, for me it was the equivalent of bussing a never-ending nut when I was riding my man. I squinted slightly when the sun hit my pupils, tossing my long black strands out of my view while I walked to the curb.

Rafiq mounted his Yamaha first, followed by me and Algierion. I revved the motor on my bike and had the dual pipes screaming by the time our bikes roared down the side street. Feeling the vibration from the motorcycle between my legs had my confidence on a thousand; I was dizzy from the anticipation of the rush I'd have once this job was completed. We got to the stop light and I turned on my blinker to turn left, adjusting my helmet before we turned down the street with the small café.

Leaning into the turn as my bike tilted to the left, I smiled when I saw our target sitting outside enjoying a drink with two more of my enemies. My mission was validated when I saw that there were no witnesses, inside or out. Sliding the pistol from behind my back, I giggled lightly to myself feeling the familiar pattern in my palm as I slid my finger against the trigger and screwed on the silencer. Rafiq was in front of me putting on a show in the upper-class neighborhood, spinning in circles on his bike while the women at the table shook their heads at his antics.

He saw me first, leaping to his feet while the two women at the table screamed wildly. "Long live the Queen, muthafucka!" I screamed out as Algierion and Rafiq did doughnuts in the middle of the street on either side of me. Aiming the laser at my target I tugged on the pistol's trigger five times, first shooting both women in the chest twice before putting a bullet in the center of his forehead. I watched as his body froze for a second before tipping over to crash through the glass table. Nodding my head with satisfaction, I signaled my team before we all revved our bikes again and took off doing 90 MPH down the small side street at the sirens whined in the distance.

*

"I'm confused on why this shop," I smacked a stack of papers off the counter as the store manager looked at me sideways, "is the one shop in this entire fucking city that's not turning a profit!" After we killed the bastard that tried taking over my number one block that I made money on, my energy was still high, so I made a stop at one of my auto shops. Although the shop was always packed, for some reason they always reported a loss in sales at the end of the month.

"Yasmine you gotta understand—" the big man huffed up in my face, raising his voice. I don't know why these men confused me with some weak bitch who would go cower in a corner because they had bass in their voice and I didn't.

"No Neef, YOU gotta understand that Yasmine Perez ain't with the shits. All my businesses make money and when they ain't making me money, I cut that shit off!"

"Oh, so you jus' gonna close this shop?" he took two steps closer to where I stood. "See this why we ain't making no money, you don't know what the fuck you doin'!"

"I never said I was closing the shop, asshole! I said I was cutting some shit off, bitch!" I pulled my pistol from the small of my back and shot him dead center in the dome. "RAFIQ! Clean this shit up!"

"Ya-Ya you can't just be out here shooting everybody that piss you off," Algierion eased up behind me, wrapping his arms around me as he peck-kissed me on my neck with his dick pressed against my back. "Why you so tense?"

"Let's go home, I'm ready to wind down." I reached around and rubbed his head as his hand found my sweet spot.

"Aye, who gonna run the shop since you killed this nigga?" Rafiq yelled out to no one, pulling Neef's dead body to his office in the back.

"Hell, somebody in here trying to get promoted," I looked around the shop and saw the mechanics focused on the cars in their bays, not paying us no attention. "Him." I pointed at an older man focused on diagnosing the car in front of him. "Every time I walk in here, he busy. He can run the shop."

Rafiq closed the door to the office before he stepped inside the shop and spoke lowly to the older man. Nodding his head as he pointed at me, the older man paused for a second before clasping his hands in front of his face and bowing slightly in my direction. *Thank you,* he mouthed as I nodded back.

"Let's go home so I can take care of that business real quick," Algierion whispered in my ear, rubbing the curve of my booty. "You gonna give me a baby?"

"Not tonight," I switched my ass out of the shop with him walking behind me, still pressed against my frame. "Look at how these leggings hugging my pussy."

"Lemme hug yo' pussy," Algierion smacked my ass as I climbed on my motorcycle. "Then you can ride this dick for the rest of the night, aight?"

"Fuck you, Algierion," I giggled at him hopping behind me on my bike, mashing his thickness against my booty cheeks as he pulled my head back by my hair. "Stop!"

"Naw, I'ma go." He sped up his dry humping on my back with his meat about to stab a hole in my side. "Fuck me back Ya-Ya."

"Let's go home so I can cool yo' hot ass off." I pushed him off my bike with a hard dick and a smile. "I know how to get a baaaag, don't I? I know how to make 'em maaaad, don't I?"

"Getcho ass home before you piss me off!" Algierion yelled, waiting until I pulled off first before he came up behind me. Racing down Lake Shore Drive to our brownstone in Lincoln Park, I parked in the garage and kicked off my boots as he pulled in behind me, stripping off my clothes while running upstairs. I couldn't wait until he gave me...

"Ya-Ya! Daddy's home!"

Connect with Fatima Munroe

Website

www.fatimasbooks.com

Social Media

Facebook: http://facebook.com/authorfatimamunroe

http://facebook.com/groups/ReadingWithFatima

Twitter: http://twitter.com/fatima_munroe

Instagram: http://instagram.com/fatima_munroe

YouTube: http://bit.ly/Munroe20

Read a book by me? Start here:

Married To A Chicago Bully series: http://amzn.to/2uWoyAs

Taste: An Erotic Novella: https://amzn.to/2DnfPOj

Never Make A Promise- A Valentine Love Story:
http://amzn.to/2o5TNVc

Pretty Gurls Love Savages (Book 1 of 3): https://amzn.to/2W2T872

Don't forget to leave a review!

Fatima Munroe